# NOT IN THE PINK

A PARANORMAL COZY MYSTERY

A WITCH'S COVE MYSTERY
BOOK FIVE

VELLA DAY

EROTIC READS PUBLISHING

Copyright © 2020 Vella Day

www.velladay.com

velladayauthor@gmail.com

Edited by Rebecca Cartee and Carol Adcock-Bezzo

Published in the United States of America

E-book ISBN: 978-1-951430-14-6

Print book ISBN: 978-1-951430-15-3

ALL RIGHTS RESERVED. No part of this book may be used or reproduced in any manner whatsoever without written permission of the author except in the case of brief questions embodied in critical articles or reviews.

This is a work of fiction. Names, characters, places, and incidents either are the product of the author's imagination or are used fictitiously, and any resemblance to actual persons living or dead, business establishments, events or locales, is entirely coincidental.

# ABOUT THE BOOK

**A pink iguana convinced he can talk to a cat ghost. A woman's psychic vision leading to another murder. And a witch who has no idea who to believe.**

Hi, I'm Glinda Goodall, part-time witch and part-time amateur sleuth from Witch's Cove, Florida, a beach town full of witches and gossips.

Iggy--my talking pink iguana--just dropped a bomb on me, saying he just communicated with the ghost of some widow's pet. I might have dismissed that nonsense if the man didn't die the next day--just as this ghost cat had predicted! Now Iggy is determined to solve his murder, with or without my help.

I was losing faith that anyone would ever need my services as an amateur sleuth, when a high-profile woman shows up to our office claiming she had a vision of her husband being murdered and wants me to look into it. The problem? He's not dead. The sheriff dismissed her case, but that only gives me more reason to help her.

Things get really weird when her husband actually is

murdered, and guess who's the number one suspect? You guessed it. This woman. There goes my first paying customer. I won't abandoned her though. I'm determined to prove she's innocent.

When I'm not running around looking for clues, I waitress at the Tiki Hut Grill, so stop in for a smile and a great cup of coffee--or just to check in to see where I am in solving the case.

# CHAPTER 1

Hi, I'm Glinda Goodall, co-owner of The Pink Iguana Sleuths. We aren't doing any investigating right now since we can't seem to land any paying clients, but we are not giving up.

So, while we wait for someone to come knocking on our door, I've gone back to waitressing at my aunt's restaurant, the Tiki Hut Grill. Jaxson Harrison, my partner in this new business, has been earning a little extra cash loading wine for his brother who owns the Cheese and Wine Emporium located below our office.

Phew. That about sums up my life—well, almost. Now for the present.

After finishing a double shift at the restaurant, I was seriously in need of a solid eight hours of sleep. I dragged my tired body up the rear restaurant staircase and entered my apartment. Just as I was about to take off my pink bejeweled crown that was part of my waitress costume—as Glinda the Good Witch of the South, of course—my familiar, a pink iguana, jumped off his stool and charged.

I expected the little bugger to stop at my feet and do some

sort of excitement dance, but instead, he scrambled up my legs, shocking me when he grabbed my cheeks with his rather sharp claws and looked me in the eye.

Even though we'd been together fourteen years, he'd never done anything like that before. My surprise caused me to grab a hold of him with two hands and then hold him out at arm's length. "What in the world has gotten into you?"

"I saw a ghost! I saw a ghost!" His excitement had my own heart beating hard.

Okay, a normal person would either dismiss this as some kind of hallucination or be totally shocked at the existence of ghosts. Me? Neither was the case. You see, a few months ago, I too had seen and spoken to a ghost—or rather to two ghosts. And yes, my iguana can talk.

Before I continue about my familiar's newest revelation, I need to backtrack, because it will explain why it was reasonable to believe he could talk to a ghost. The reason Iggy ended up pink was because at the ripe old age of twelve, in the process of conjuring him, I messed up my spell. Shock, right? I often goofed up my spells.

Anyway, my theory was that since I only wore pink, my infatuation with the color must have caused him to change from green to pink. Being male, it embarrassed him, and I couldn't blame the poor little guy.

After years of him pestering me, I finally found a spell to change him back. The problem was that the witch who collected the ingredients became a bit preoccupied during the process and gave me one wrong ingredient. At the time, we were unaware of the glitch and drank the potion.

Instead of Iggy returning to his natural green state, we both ended up with the ability to see ghosts. Luckily for the first ghost we encountered, we were able to help him with the identity of the person who had murdered him.

Iggy wiggled in my hands. "Did you hear what I just said?" he asked not so nicely.

"You saw a ghost, did you? Was it Morgan Oliver again?" He was our first ghost.

"No. It was the ghost of a cat."

If I had been drinking tea, I might have spit it all over him. "A cat? Wow. I need a drink. Let's go into the kitchen, and you can tell me all about it."

Iggy had a lot of flaws, but out and out lying wasn't one of them. He did exaggerate—sometimes a lot—but he wouldn't make up something this important. I placed him on the two-person kitchen table and then grabbed a glass from the cabinet.

"While you were working—all day, I might add—I had nothing to do," Iggy said.

That was his usual ploy for sympathy. "Did you visit Aimee?"

Aimee was the black cat who lived across the hall with my aunt. Due to circumstances beyond Aimee's control, the same witch who messed up the potion that was supposed to return Iggy to green, accidentally gave Aimee the ability to speak. Iggy fancies himself her boyfriend, but too often she ignores him. And that causes him to be sad and sometimes rebellious.

"No, she wasn't home." For once, he didn't sound upset.

"What did you do instead?" I asked.

"I went outside. I hadn't even reached the beach boardwalk when I felt a rush of cold air pass by me. Since I'd felt the same thing with Mr. Oliver—the ghost we helped—I figure he'd returned."

"That's logical, but the last time I communicated with him, he said he would be passing over now that he had no unfinished business."

"I remember. It turns out it wasn't Morgan Oliver. Before

I could figure out what was happening, this beautiful gray Persian cat blocks my way."

"Persian?"

"Yes. Her name is Sassy, but she wasn't nearly as transparent as Uncle Henry had been—or Morgan Oliver, for that matter. When I reached out to touch her, though, I felt nothing but air. It was creepy."

This was intriguing. I poured myself a glass of sweet iced tea and sat down at the kitchen table. "Was she able to communicate with you?"

"Yes, and here's the strange part. She isn't anyone's familiar."

"Then she couldn't talk." At least I was led to believe that only familiars had the power of speech—unless they were accidentally given the power, like Aimee had been.

"That's the thing. I'm an animal. She's an animal. While I can't talk to a random dog, I guess once an animal has crossed the rainbow bridge, they are given the power to communicate with familiars—at least that's my best guess."

"For real?"

"Of course, for real. How else would I know her name?"

I tossed back part of my drink. "Did Sassy say anything of interest?"

"Not at first. She was so thrilled to find someone who could hear her that she asked *me* a lot of questions."

"How long ago did she pass?"

Iggy tilted his head. "I don't know. Who cares? She's dead now."

I would have thought he'd have become a better detective than that by now. "Did you bother to find out whose pet she was?"

He scratched his face. I always thought it meant he was trying to recall a detail. "Yes. Before she *passed*, she belonged to Chester Hightower."

My heart went out to him. "He owns the Witch's Cove movie theater that I love."

My partner, Jaxson, had told me a few months back there was a rumor going around stating that someone wanted to buy the building, tear it down, and convert it into condos. While having a condo overlooking the Gulf of Mexico in sunny Florida would be wonderful for the occupants, it would be terrible for lovers of old movies. The memories I'd shared with friends at that theater had been immense.

"I know," Iggy said.

"I'm sorry to hear of his loss." Those words just tumbled out. That came as no surprise since my parents owned the Cove Funeral home.

"She said he was really sad about it."

"I can only imagine. Did she say anything else?"

"Yes. Sassy is really worried about Chester," Iggy said.

Sometimes Iggy could draw out a story way too long. "About what? Is his health failing?" The man had to be at least eighty.

"He thinks someone is trying to kill him."

I sucked in a breath. "No way. Does she know who?"

"No, but his theater is losing money, and his son, along with his deceased son's wife have been pressuring him to sell it to some big-time developer."

"I hope he doesn't give in. I know I'm often too tired to go to the movies, but when I do, the classics move me."

"Apparently, not enough people feel the same way."

"Now you're an expert?" That snarky comment wasn't called for, but hearing that Chester Hightower was having troubles upset me.

"No worse than you." He turned his snout toward me, which meant he wasn't looking at me since his eyes were on the side of his head. That was his passive aggressive stance.

"Make me feel bad, why don't you? Maybe you can ask

Sassy to return to her old haunt and find out who wants him dead."

"I suggested that, but she said being back home might creep her out."

"Seriously? I didn't know cats cared enough." To be honest, I knew very little about cats and their feelings.

"I did ask her who she thought wanted him dead."

"And?" I asked.

"She didn't know for sure, but she doesn't trust either the widowed daughter-in-law or his son, Darren."

"Really? Darren Hightower, who runs the theater, is a nice guy. According to several knowledgeable people, he's donated his time and money to many good causes."

"He might be a saint, but that doesn't mean he didn't urge old dad to sell. That property would bring the family a lot of money, I bet."

"You're right. I remember when Darren's brother died three years ago. The rumor mill claimed he didn't leave his wife, Amanda, with a ton of money."

"See? Both Mr. Hightower's daughter-in-law and son have a motive to want the old guy dead," Iggy said. "As for me? I just want to help Sassy."

His interest seemed to be more than a desire to help. "Do you like this ghost cat or something?"

"She's pretty, for sure."

"Iggy Goodall. You have a girlfriend. What about Aimee?"

"What about her?"

I wasn't sure how to answer. Clearly, I had failed to raise him responsibly. "Fidelity is one of the most important components in a relationship."

He lifted his chest. "I'm trying to be a good person. Don't worry. I am fully aware that Sassy is dead, which means it's not like I can actually have any physical contact with her. I'm betting I never see her again. I think she only appeared to ask me to help find the person who was after Mr. Hightower."

Iggy really seemed to want to help. "How about if I speak with him? I'll ask Jaxson to do a little digging into who wants to buy the theater and for how much. I'm betting Mr. Hightower himself has an idea who might be targeting him."

Iggy jumped up and down. "Yes, thank you." He scurried off the table and ran out of the kitchen.

"Where are you going?"

"To tell Sassy the good news."

I jumped up from the table and dashed after him. "You said you didn't know how to contact her."

"I never said that." With that, my precious iguana was out the cat door.

I suppose that since ghosts don't sleep, she might be hanging about. As for me? I needed to go to bed. Tomorrow, I wasn't working at the restaurant, which would give me time to discuss our new pro bono case with Jaxson and see how he wanted to handle it.

Since Iggy could take care of himself, I headed to my bedroom, despite my mind spinning. I know one thing I could do to help—put a protection spell around Mr. Hightower to keep away the evil until Jaxson and I could figure out who wanted the man dead.

# CHAPTER 2

The next morning, I found Jaxson in his brother's wine shop doing inventory. He looked up and smiled. "Hey, pink lady. You off today?"

"Yes, thank goodness, but I will not be idle."

"What are you planning to do?"

"I'm going to do some detecting work, with your help, of course."

Jaxson closed the laptop and gave me his undivided attention. "Don't tell me we have a case?"

"Pro bono."

He chuckled. "Is there any other kind?"

I had to admit that I never expected Jaxson to be so laid back about our new business. His philosophy was that with each case we solved—whether it was for money or not—we would learn something. And learning was needed if we were to become successful.

"Probably not for a while. Anyway, last night when I returned from work, Iggy rushed up to me."

"Don't tell me he and Aimee had a date."

I laughed. We both understood how one-sided that love affair was. "No. In fact, he saw a ghost of a cat."

I shouldn't have been surprised that my partner was rather speechless, despite believing both Iggy and I had previously communicated with ghosts. "A cat ghost?"

"Yes." I explained about Sassy being Mr. Hightower's deceased pet and that she was worried because someone wanted to kill him.

"That is intriguing. I'm assuming Mr. Hightower has proof of these threats?"

"That's what I want to find out."

Jaxson dipped his chin. "You want to investigate this? There's not been a crime."

"I know, but I owe Iggy to at least see if what this ghost said was true. What if someone harmed old Mr. Hightower, and we did nothing to stop it?"

Jaxson smiled and shook his head. "You are incorrigible."

"Great. You agree to help." He hadn't, but I assumed he would. "Could you look into Mr. Hightower's family? He has a widowed daughter-in-law—a Mrs. Amanda Hightower—who I heard is hurting for money. Mr. Hightower's younger son, Darren, runs the theater. He'd know more than anyone the financial strength of the company."

"Can do. And you?"

"I want to speak with Mr. Hightower to see if he's been threatened or if this is merely a case of an old man being paranoid. If he has evidence, did he call the sheriff's department?"

"Why not just ask Steve?"

"You know the sheriff would just tell me to leave things alone."

"True. Okay, while you speak with Mr. Hightower, I'll do a little computer snooping."

"You are the best."

He lifted his hand. "That's why I wear my pink wristband. It gives me my super powers." Jaxson winked.

He also owned pink socks, a pink T-shirt—which was a bit too matchy-matchy for me—and pink briefs, ones he revealed to me one time.

"You go, Superman."

Jaxson laughed. "Good luck."

Before I contacted Mr. Hightower, I headed to the Hex and Bones Apothecary Shop to learn what I needed for a protection spell. If Mr. Hightower was indisposed or refused to talk with me, the least I could do was put the spell around his front door.

Inside the shop, I found Bertha, the owner, helping a customer. While I waited for her to be free, I checked out the stack of books along the west wall that contained many spells. I could have consulted Gertrude Poole about which spell would be the most effective one to use since she was the most experienced witch in town, but I didn't want to bother her unless I had to.

"Glinda," Bertha said.

I turned around. "Hey, Bertha."

"It's good to see you again. Any more ghost sightings?"

It had been her assistant who had blended the ingredients incorrectly that caused my ability to manifest itself in the first place. "Nope. Not yet."

Even though she was very open-minded, I didn't see the need to tell her about Iggy spotting a ghost.

"What can I do for you?"

"I'm looking for a protection spell."

"For yourself?"

"No. I can't give you many details, but it's for a case I'm working on. Someone suspects his life is in danger."

"Oh, no." She looked genuinely concerned.

"I want to put a spell either on his house or directly on

him, if that is possible, to ward off any evil."

"Of course. I have just the thing."

I followed her to the counter where Bertha gathered five ingredients. "Where can I find the spell for this?" I asked.

Usually, I wasn't this impatient, but I feared I'd mess things up if everything wasn't laid out perfectly for me. It didn't matter that the last few spells—one of which enabled Jaxson to communicate with Iggy—had worked. I also had figured out how to cloak myself, but the side effects to invisibility made it such that I might never do it again.

"Let me get that for you." She ducked into the back room and returned shortly with a printout of the spell. It was in plain English and sounded simple enough.

"Here, we go," Bertha said. "You'll need a small cooking plate too. Just add these powders to water and boil it. Say the spell and let the smoke do the rest of the work!"

"Smoke?" I doubted Mr. Hightower would appreciate that.

"Just a little smoke. Wave your hands to disperse it if it's too much."

This was sounding a bit dangerous. He might have breathing problems. "Is this safe?"

"Of course. I've performed the spell several times. It will ward off all evil for days."

I could work with that. After I paid, I sat in my car—with the engine running so I didn't die from the Florida heat—and studied what I needed to do. Clearly, I had to return home to collect the cooking plate before contacting Mr. Hightower. Once I was able to recite the spell without stumbling, I rushed home.

As soon as I stepped inside my apartment, Iggy jumped off his stool that overlooked the ocean and came over. "What did you find out?" he asked.

"I haven't spoken to Mr. Hightower yet." I explained about

the protection spell.

"A spell?" He sounded doubtful.

"Yes, a spell. Don't worry, Bertha said it was an easy one. I can't get it wrong."

"Uh-huh."

I didn't need any of his attitude today. Doing magic always made me nervous. "Did you find Sassy?"

He dropped onto his stomach. "No. She wouldn't come out."

I hated to see him frustrated. And here I thought he knew for sure where she would be. "How about when I'm talking to Mr. Hightower, I ask him about her favorite haunts? Maybe she's there."

He lifted his head. "Would you?"

"Sure." I gathered my matches and my Sterno cooking pot and placed them in my large bag along with the other ingredients. "Wish me luck."

"You'll be great," he said.

His cheerful response surprised and delighted me. "Thank you."

I'd already looked up Mr. Hightower's address and found that he lived in one of the more affluent neighborhoods several blocks from the ocean. I thought about calling him first, but I didn't want him to tell me to leave him alone.

While he used to come into the restaurant on a regular basis, of late, I hadn't seen him. I hoped that didn't mean he had taken ill. Even if he was well, he might not recognize me without my Glinda the Good Witch costume.

Since I wasn't very good with directions, I used an app on my phone to find his place. He lived in a lovely home, one that was well kept up. I was happy for him. What I wasn't pleased about was the lack of security. Anyone could sneak up to his place without notice. He probably figured he didn't need to install a fence since this was Witch's Cove, where there wasn't much crime—other than a few murders here and there.

I rang the bell and waited. It seemed to take forever before the door opened. To my delight, Mr. Hightower, a tall, thin, white-haired man answered. For someone his age though, he sure looked in the pink—that was, in the picture of health.

"Hello, Mr. Hightower. Remember me? I'm Glinda from the Tiki Hut Grill."

It took him a moment before the light came to his eyes. "Glinda. Yes, yes. Come in. Sorry. I don't get many visitors."

I would have thought his daughter-in-law or son would check up on him on a regular basis, but I'd ask about them later. "Thank you."

I followed him to the living room. "Can I get you some tea?" he asked.

While I loved tea, I didn't want to put him out. "I'm good, thanks."

He sat down. "How can I help you?"

Now came for the hard part. Our town was known for its witches, but not all residents were believers. "I know this may sound very odd, but do you remember my pink iguana, Iggy?"

"Oh, yes. Cute fellow."

"He is. Iggy is also very talented. He told me that he saw your Sassy yesterday."

Mr. Hightower shook his head and his hands trembled. "That's not possible. Sassy passed away two weeks ago."

That gave me a timeline for her death. "I know, but she came back in her ghost form." I held up a hand. "Before you say that's crazy, please hear me out. I can sometimes see ghosts too, but I can't see Sassy for some reason. I think only very special animals can."

His lips pressed together. "Come into the kitchen with me

while I make some tea. I think I'm going to need it."

"You might." I followed him once more and perched onto one of the high-top stools at the counter. "I can't make you believe me, but when Sassy spoke to Iggy, she said she was worried about you."

He filled the kettle with water and then placed it on the stove. "Why is that?"

I was certain Iggy hadn't made this up. "She said you believed someone was trying to kill you."

He spun around so fast, I feared he'd knock over the kettle. "That's unbelievable. I mean, I confided everything to that cat. Are you telling me she understood me all these years?"

"Apparently."

He shuffled over to a cabinet where he withdrew a teabag and a cup. "Are you sure you wouldn't like a cup?"

"Now that you're making it, I would."

He pulled down a second cup and retrieved an additional teabag from a container. "I'm not sure if you've heard, but a large developer is trying to buy the theater."

"I had heard the rumors, but I'm guessing you aren't keen on selling?"

"No. After I die, if Amanda or my son, Darren, want to sell, then so be it."

The sooner he died, the sooner they'd get their inheritance though. Maybe one of them would be interested in hurrying up the inevitable.

"Have there been any attempts on your life to make you think you are in danger?"

"No one has attacked me, but I received a note saying that if I didn't sell, I'd die."

Whoa. That certainly counted as evidence. "Really? May I see this note?"

"I gave it to the sheriff, but I made a copy." He flashed me

NOT IN THE PINK | 15

a charming smile.

"Smart."

He walked out, presumably to find the copy. When the water boiled, and he hadn't returned, I fixed the two cups of tea and placed them on the counter to steep. My heart saddened a bit at the delicate porcelain cups. The pink and green flowers painted on the side looked like the ones my grandmother used to own.

"Here it is," Mr. Hightower said.

He handed me a scanned document that showed a message cut out in letters from a magazine. "I see. I didn't realize people even read magazines anymore."

"My daughter-in-law does."

Interesting. "Did you tell Steve about that? I mean Sheriff Rocker?"

"No, he didn't ask."

I removed my teabag and sipped the too hot tea. "Who do you think sent it?"

He shrugged. "I can only think of three people."

"Are Amanda or Darren two of those people?"

Mr. Hightower nodded. "It's also possible the note came from Loughlin Merriman, the developer."

"I can understand why you'd think it was him, but your own family?"

"I know. It sickens me to consider them, but Amanda just can't live within her means. When my son, Tim, was alive, he provided well enough for her. After his death, she made some unwise investment choices."

"I'm sorry. I assume she is in favor of you selling the theater?"

"Of course, but the money would have been mine, not hers."

"And Darren?" I asked.

"He runs the theater. I always thought he loved it, but of

late he's been reminding me just how much it's costing me to keep it open. I just can't bear to close it though."

"I get it. I love watching the old movies there."

"So do I." He sighed.

I snapped my fingers. "I'm not sure why this matters anymore, but Iggy wants to talk to Sassy again, only he can't find her. Is there any place she likes to go?"

"She was an indoor cat."

"Oh." I drank more of my tea, now that it had cooled a bit. "How mad was Mr. Merriman that you wouldn't sell?"

Mr. Hightower seemed to think about that. "He was never angry exactly. Just persistent. I guess he figured his time would come. Eventually, I'd die and then he could buy the property."

"Didn't Loughlin Merriman build the Beachside Condos in town?"

"He did."

I would have thought one condo on the beach would have been enough. "Just in case someone does try something, would you mind if I put a protection spell around you?"

He huffed out a laugh. "A protection spell?"

"It's not hocus pocus. It works. I promise. It will keep evil at bay."

Mr. Hightower held up his hands and chuckled. "It can't hurt, right?"

"No. Since you don't plan on selling, we need to make sure you stay safe."

"Thank you, Glinda. I appreciate your support."

I moved over to the small kitchen table where I unpacked my herbs, along with the metal dish that I would use to burn them. I then explained the process. "Once I light the Sterno, it will start to boil the liquid and herbs. I'll say the spell, and then we'll be done."

He inhaled. "I'm ready."

## CHAPTER 3

When I returned from putting the protection spell on Mr. Hightower, I found Jaxson upstairs in our office.

"Did you find out anything about the Hightower family?" I asked, setting my backpack purse on my desk.

"Not much. Neither the daughter-in-law nor the son have a record."

Too bad. That would have made things easier. "Mr. Hightower's eldest son died three years ago. By any chance, did you find out about the circumstances of his death? His son couldn't have been very old."

Jaxson typed something in his computer. "It says here that he died in a car accident."

"Was anyone charged, or was he just being careless and ran into a telephone pole?"

"Apparently, he was run off the road, but the driver of the other car never stopped."

I shuddered. I couldn't imagine living with myself if I had caused another person's death. "Three years ago, two of your favorite people were running the sheriff's office. Maybe they didn't follow up."

Jaxson's lip curled as he typed something else. "Bingo. Deputy Cliff Duncan was the officer in charge."

Darn. "That means either he didn't investigate thoroughly, or he was paid to look the other way." Since Cliff was dead, we'd never know the truth.

Jaxson faced her. "Where do we go from here?"

"I'm going to talk to Steve about the threatening note that was sent to Mr. Hightower." I should have asked if the threat came in the mail or if he found it taped to his front door or something. It could be important.

Jaxson chuckled. "And you expect our esteemed sheriff to tell you anything?"

"I do. I plan to barter Iggy's information for his."

"Other than telling you Mr. Hightower was in danger, what else does Iggy know?"

"Not much, but the sheriff has seen firsthand how valuable Iggy's intel can be. Maybe it's what he can do for him in the future that matters."

"As usual, I'll continue to look for some dirt while you covertly gather information from our men in brown."

I smiled. "While you're at it, check out Loughlin Merriman. He's the developer who wants to buy the theater." I told him how Mr. Hightower described him as persistent but not aggressive.

"Can do. I would think in order to erect a condo of any size though, he'd need more land than just where the theater is located."

"You're probably right. Didn't you tell me—or maybe it was your brother—that the developer was trying to buy the ice cream shop next to the theater too?"

He nodded. "You're right. I remember that now."

"I wonder if those two spaces would be enough."

"Could be."

"I might have to give the owner of the ice cream shop a visit."

Jaxson smiled. "You are a rolling stone, Glinda Goodall."

I laughed. "Because I let no moss gather on me?"

"Yup."

"It's the only way to get ahead in life," I said.

"Let me know what you learn."

"Will do."

Once I left Jaxson, I decided to check out the ice cream store before I headed to the sheriff's office. If there had been no threats on this owner's life, I would focus my attention on Hightower's family—and on the developer. I had to assume that Steve and Nash had already done a fair amount of investigation. Hopefully, they'd let something slip.

Next door to the theater was the shop that I spent much of my high school youth at. I went inside and ordered a mint chocolate chip ice cream cone. A girl needed her energy, right? Sandy Eaton, the manager, was there. While she wasn't the owner, she might know what was going on with the prospective sale.

"Hey, Sandy, do you have a minute?"

The manager looked around. Since I was the only one in the store, she'd be hard pressed to say no. "Sure."

"I was talking to Mr. Hightower this morning, and he said that Merriman Developers wants to buy this property, as well as the land the theater sits on, to build a condo. Did you know about that?"

"I did."

Darn. "I'm sorry." I meant it.

"Me, too. I've been here forever, but I realize that times change. The place needs an overhaul, yet Mr. Plimpton doesn't want to put any more money into it. He's ready to retire and move to Connecticut where his children live."

"I get it. So, he's agreed to sell, I take it?"

"He has. Between you and me, we're lucky to break even on a monthly basis—other than in the summer. It makes sense for him to sell the shop."

"It's sad. I love this place." I looked around. "It holds so many memories.

There was no use asking if there had been any threats on Mr. Plimpton's life since he'd agreed to sell. I finished my ice cream cone and headed over to the sheriff's office. Was I a little disappointed that Mr. Plimpton's life hadn't been on the line too? Maybe. It would have taken the focus off of Mr. Hightower's family. Oh, well. No one said this sleuthing business was going to be easy.

The current problem was that I didn't have much information to offer the sheriff. He already knew about Hightower's death threat note. It was possible the sheriff would ask Iggy to do a little research—assuming Sassy actually knew anything else—but that request might be more to please me than to learn anything.

If Sassy understood that a little snooping would help her owner, she might be willing to check things out on her own. If no one could see her, she'd be the perfect sleuth.

When I entered the sheriff's department, Pearl, Steve's grandmother, shoved her knitting needles in the drawer. Instead of her usual cheerful greeting, she wouldn't meet my gaze.

"Pearl, are you okay?"

"Sure. Peachy. How can I help you?"

Pearl was never curt. "I'd like to speak with Steve."

Pearl leaned back in her seat and finally looked at me, her frown rather disconcerting. "He's not here. Are you here to turn yourself in?"

"Turn myself in? What are you talking about?"

"Steve and Nash went over to your office to find you."

Pearl wasn't making any sense. "What for?"

"To arrest you."

I laughed. I mean, how could I not? "Arrest me for what?"

"For murdering Mr. Hightower."

"What? He's dead?" My legs nearly gave way. Pearl must have recognized my dire situation and jumped up to help—or should I say, she got out of her chair as fast as she could for someone her age.

She took hold of my arm and led me to a seat against the wall. "Let me get you some water."

Did that mean she didn't think I was guilty? Or was she trying to keep me there until Steve returned? I probably should have assured her I wasn't planning on going anywhere.

When she remained out of sight for a bit too long, I figured Pearl was in his office calling him. It didn't matter. I wanted to speak with him. If nothing else, I had to clear my name.

No sooner had Pearl returned with a glass of water than Steve and Nash rushed in, both looking rather upset.

"Glinda," Steve said in a voice I'd never heard him use before.

I sat up straighter. I wasn't going to be intimidated. "Sheriff Rocker."

"We've been looking for you. Let's speak in my office."

My heart remained firmly lodged in my stomach as I stood on wobbly legs. Thankfully, he hadn't slapped cuffs on me. How could he possibly believe I had anything to do with Mr. Hightower's death? The fact someone killed him right after I visited the man really upset me. My protection spell had failed—and to think Bertha swore it would work. The sad part was that I had followed her instructions to the letter. I really was a bad witch after all.

Without saying another word, I entered his office. He

motioned I sit across from his desk while Nash sat next to me. Did they really think they needed two officers to keep me corralled? Sheesh.

From the deputy's stern countenance, it was like he'd already convicted me.

"What were you doing at Mr. Hightower's home earlier today?" Steve asked.

"How do you know I was there?"

"Someone saw you."

I should have asked who, but it didn't matter who had tattled. "You might find this hard to believe, but I went to his house to warn him."

"About what?" Nash asked.

I inhaled. "It all started when Iggy spoke to Mr. Hightower's dead cat."

Let them figure that one out.

"And how did he do that?" Steve asked with a straight face.

"Mr. Hightower's cat, whose name was Sassy, appeared to Iggy as a ghost."

He failed to keep his eyebrows from rising. "I see. Did you speak with this ghost too?"

"No. I've not had any sightings since my uncle passed over."

Steve pulled out that stupid yellow pad of his from his desk drawer and jotted down something. "Then what?"

I went through the whole series of events, from asking Jaxson to research the daughter-in-law and the son, to me going to the Hex and Bones Apothecary shop for the ingredients for a protection spell. "You can ask Bertha about the spell. She'll vouch for me."

Steve scribbled that down. "We will, though clearly this spell didn't work."

"I realize that." He didn't need to rub my failure in my face.

"Then what did you do?"

"I went to Mr. Hightower's house and told him that his cat was worried about him."

"Did he believe you that his pet had come back from the dead to speak to Iggy?"

And here I thought Steve was a believer in the occult. Iggy had proven himself time and again to be a reliable source. "He did, in part because I knew about the death threat. Mr. Hightower told me that he'd shown you the letter with the cut up message." Before he asked another question, I rushed on. "What he failed to tell you was that his daughter reads a lot of magazines. Did you question her?"

"We did. She was with Darren, her brother-in-law, at the time of Mr. Hightower's death."

How convenient. "Can anyone confirm that?"

"Glinda, this is our case. Please do not interfere."

That was rich. "You accuse me of murder even though I barely know the man and then say to stay out of it?"

Steve glanced over at Nash and then back at me. "That is exactly what I'm saying."

"What proof do you have that I might have killed Mr. Hightower?"

Once more they glanced at each other. "That's confidential."

"Ah ha. That means you have nothing. Mr. Hightower and I drank some tea, I did the spell, and then I left. I was feeling rather confident that he would be safe for at least a few days, though now I realize my spell didn't work. Before you ask where I went next, I headed straight to the office to ask Jaxson to look into Loughlin Merriman."

"Why would you need to investigate him?"

Why? I thought it was quite obvious, but maybe Steve

wanted a second opinion. "Because he was the one who was pressuring Mr. Hightower to sell the theater so he could build some stupid condo on the beach. The owner of the ice cream shop has already agreed to sell."

"I see." More notes.

What did that mean? "Can you at least tell me how Mr. Hightower died?" I held out my hands. "You can test for gunshot residue if you want."

I swear his lips almost quirked up. "He wasn't shot."

"Was he poisoned? I poured the tea while he was locating a copy of the death threat." I placed my purse on the counter. "You can look in here for any poison."

"Glinda, please. Let us do our job."

"Your job? You need to talk to his daughter-in-law again, as well as to Mr. Merriman."

"We will."

So far, they hadn't said I was under arrest. "Pearl told me you were going to arrest me."

His brows pinched. "Since when do you ever listen to my grandmother?"

Often. The gossip queens were the main source of my knowledge about murder and such. "So now what?"

"Tell me this. What was Mr. Hightower's health like? Did he complain of chest pains or anything?"

Those questions were telling. "No. He looked to be in peak physical condition—or at least as good as you can be when you're in your eighties."

"And his mental state?" Steve asked.

"I was a bit disappointed he wasn't more concerned about the threat."

"Yet he let you do this protection spell, right?"

"Yes, but I think he was just humoring me. He seemed like a lonely man who appreciated my company."

"I see."

When neither produced any cuffs, I figured I wasn't going to land in jail today. "Am I free to go?"

Nash placed a hand on my arm. "Yes, but don't leave town, and please don't investigate."

Like that was going to happen. "Whatever you say."

Even though Steve released me, I was shaken. Bad. In need of a pick-me-up, I went next door to the Bubbling Cauldron Coffee shop. I wasn't going for the gossip this time but rather for a strong cup of coffee and something sweet. Sure, if Miriam knew anything about Mr. Hightower's death, I would listen. No doubt Pearl had called all of the gossip queens the moment she learned Mr. Hightower had passed.

No sooner had I snagged a table near the window than Miriam rushed over. "Glinda, did you hear?"

I admit it. My pulse soared. Gossip was the lifeblood of a detective—or rather for an amateur sleuth. "Hear what?"

Playing dumb usually worked better than being a know-it-all.

"Chester Hightower died this morning."

I couldn't lie, especially since Pearl knew what had happened and had probably already called to say Steve suspected me! Those two were thick as thieves. The problem was that my Aunt Fern would know too. I just hoped she didn't call my mother and tell her before I could. Mom would be worried sick. "I had heard that. Any idea how he died?"

"Pearl thinks it was a heart attack."

I was about to say that was unlikely since the man had received a death threat, but I didn't want it to get back to the sheriff that I was spreading rumors. If Steve believed Mr. Hightower had died from natural causes, he wouldn't have questioned me about his death. "Who found the body?"

That was something I should have asked him. Mr. Hightower said he rarely had any visitors.

"His daughter-in-law."

"How sad." Or did she see me leave his house and consider it a good opportunity to kill him? His death would ease her financial problems for a long time. Besides, it would have been easy to report his death while pretending to be the grieving relative.

"I know, right," Miriam said. "Maybe it's for the best."

Whoa. "Why is that?"

"The man was in debt up to his eyeballs with that theater. I'm sure the stress of losing something so dear was what killed him."

"Maybe."

Miriam waved a hand. "I'm sure you came in here to eat and not chat."

"It's always nice to do both." I ordered my usual coffee along with a pastry. I often let Miriam pick the sweet since she had the best taste. She also knew which pastries were my favorites.

"Be right back."

I debated calling Jaxson and telling him I was almost arrested again, but I had to talk to my mother first. If anyone could find out how Mr. Hightower had died, it would be her. She'd just ask her good friend, the medical examiner.

## CHAPTER 4

As I entered my parents' funeral home through the back entrance, I realized that if Mr. Hightower actually died of a heart attack, there would be no murder investigation, though I wondered whether there would be an autopsy. I would think so considering the threatening letter, but families around here seemed to have a say in such matters.

My mother was on the phone when I neared her office. Her door was ajar, and for once, her cairn terrier, Toto, wasn't around, barking up a storm. Either Toto was sleeping, or Dad was taking her for a walk.

I decided to wait in the hallway until my mom finished her call. My mom sighed her sister's name rather loudly. Oh, no. That wasn't good.

As much as I tried not to listen to the conversation between my mother and her younger sister, Tricia, when she raised her voice, I stiffened. Tricia was the embarrassment of the family. Mom was forty-eight and Aunt Tricia was thirty-nine. That age difference turned out to be huge in the big scheme of things, because when their dad died, Tricia was only twelve. At twenty-one, my mother was often asked to take care of her sister since their mom was forced to take on a second job.

Having the sisters interact so often might have created a tight bond between them—except it didn't. The two sisters ended up being very, very different. My mom embraced her witch side, while Tricia embraced drugs as a way to keep the pain away. I was actually surprised the two were talking right now. They hadn't spoken much over the years.

Before I'd finished my musings about the past, my mom hung up. "You can come in, Glinda."

How did she know I was there? It didn't matter. I always suspected she was a bit clairvoyant. She could talk to the dead, so why not be in tune with the living?

"Hey, what's up?" I asked.

My mother's lips pinched. "I'm sure you heard me raise my voice. That was your Aunt Tricia."

"Yes. Is she asking for money again?"

"Not this time."

THAT WAS GOOD, because the funeral home barely broke even each month, which meant my parents didn't have much to spare. As for me, I certainly wasn't flush with cash, especially since I kept getting involved with ghosts, missing dogs, and a dead deputy—none of whom ever paid for my help in solving their problems. "Then what did she want?"

"Have a seat," she said. "It's about your cousin."

"Did something happen to Rihanna?" My cousin was seventeen and the total opposite of me. I wore only pink; she wore only black. I used a light touch when it came to makeup. She coated her eyes and lips in black. And she was quite rebellious, though with a mother like that it was no wonder.

"She's staying out after curfew and hanging out with kids

my sister doesn't approve of, but I'm sure you didn't come here to listen to our family drama."

"I am interested."

"I know, sweetie. Forgive me for being abrupt, but the call has upset me."

That meant I shouldn't probe. Time to change the topic. "I have news." I tried to sound upbeat, but it came out sounding a bit phony.

"Oh, what's that? Are you and Jaxson dating?"

"Enough already with trying to fix me up. No, we aren't. I was almost arrested for Mr. Hightower's murder—assuming he was killed and didn't die of a heart attack."

"Glinda, really? I thought you were going to leave the murders to the sheriff's department."

What did it say when my own mother wasn't surprised I was dragged into a murder investigation? "He wasn't dead when I went to see him."

"I see, and why did you need to talk to Mr. Hightower, of all people?"

I repeated the story again about Iggy's ghost sighting and my desire to help him do what was right. "After I did the protection spell, I left. I thought Steve might have some insight about the death threat, but when I went there, apparently someone had seen me enter Mr. Hightower's home right before he keeled over. Steve had to question me."

"Did the sheriff think you might have killed him?"

I was so happy my mother understood. "I don't think so, but Pearl implied he did."

"Didn't you say it was a heart attack?"

"That's what Miriam thought—or rather what Pearl said she thought."

My mom shook her head. "You shouldn't believe everything those old gossips tell you."

To be honest, they usually were right. "That's partly why

I'm here. I wanted to see if you'd heard anything about his death."

Mom studied me. "I haven't. At least not yet. I'm sensing you don't think he died of a heart attack?"

"I don't."

"Are you thinking there will be an autopsy? I mean, Mr. Hightower was up in age."

"I know, but right before he died, he received a death threat." I then explained the details. "Maybe when you get the body, I can do my gem analysis on him—assuming Dr. Sanchez isn't called into action?"

My gem analysis wasn't foolproof, but when I ran my faux pink diamond necklace over a body, my magic made the stone change colors according to what killed the person. Usually, the cause of death was pretty obvious, but there had been times when the medical examiner missed something.

"Of course, sweetie. We have nothing to lose."

"Thank you. Do you think maybe you could call our medical examiner and ask if there will be an autopsy?"

"Oh, Glinda, you know I don't like to disturb her for something so trivial. When the body arrives, it will be evident if she's performed one."

Pestering the medical examiner when it really served no purpose wouldn't be good. "Okay, but let me know when the body arrives."

"I will."

My mother stood, stepped over to me, and gave me a hug. That was rare for her, but I figured her sense of family was heightened after the call from her sister.

Considering the tension in the air, I was happy to get out of there. I rushed across the street to our office, and when I spotted Jaxson hovering over the computer, my mood lightened. The man always seemed happy. Mind you, that was a total one-eighty from six months ago when he first arrived in town. He'd been angry and looking for a fight.

He looked up. "What's wrong?"

Was it that obvious? I pulled out a chair. "A lot has happened since I last saw you. Let me give you the rundown." I started with finding out that the ice cream shop owner was willing to sell his place to the condo developer. "I was just going to have a casual conversation with the sheriff, but when I walked in, I learned that Chester Hightower had been murdered."

"Seriously?"

Why would he doubt me? "Okay, maybe not murdered, but he died right after I left his house—more or less."

I went into detail about my conversation with Steve and Nash and then what I learned from Miriam.

"Is the case closed then? If it was a heart attack, there was no murder."

"I know, but I'm not buying it."

Jaxson leaned back in his chair. "Of course, you're not. You think it was a hit."

"It's possible. When Mom gets the body, I'm going to use my crystal to find the real cause of death."

He chuckled. "I'm glad to see nothing stops you from getting to the bottom of things."

"Nope."

"You have a plan, right?" he asked.

My stomach grumbled, despite the pastry I just ate. "Kind of. Sort of—not really. What do you say we have lunch at the diner?"

He huffed out a laugh. "You just want to see what Dolly Andrews knows."

"What's wrong with that? I don't think her sole source of information comes from Pearl. By now, half the town will be abuzz with what happened." Dolly owned the diner and loved to gossip.

He patted his flat stomach. "I'm game."

Just as he stood, we received a knock on the door. I looked over at Jaxson. "Are you expecting anyone?"

"No."

I rushed over to the door and pulled it open. A tall, beautiful brunette, wearing a pair of white pants, black heels, and a dark gray silk sleeveless shirt stood there, her hands knitted together.

"Yes?" I asked.

"I need some help."

Since she wasn't a ghost or a lost dog, I welcomed her. Could this be our first paying customer? "Come in, come in."

Jaxson rushed over, but I didn't like the way he was looking at her. No, we weren't dating, but maybe in a few months we might. I led her over to the sofa and motioned she sit down.

"Can we offer you some water, coffee, or tea?" Jaxson asked.

Sure, we agreed we would have refreshments available for our clients, but he sounded too happy to get her something.

"Aw, that is sweet, but I'm good."

Jaxson and I sat in the chairs across from the sofa. "How can we help?" I asked.

"I'm Divinity Merriman."

My heart dropped to my stomach. "The developer's wife?"

"You've heard of him, I see."

"Yes, he plans on building a condo where the old movie theater is located."

"That's a big maybe, since Mr. Hightower hasn't agreed to sell."

She acted as if she hadn't heard about his death. "I guess you didn't know. He passed away a few hours ago."

"Oh, no. I'm so sorry."

The woman sounded sincere, but I wasn't always the best judge of character. I'd been fooled a few times in the past. "How can we help you?"

"This is a bit embarrassing, but I've had a vision."

I sat up straighter. This was up my alley. "Are you a psychic?"

"No, but it's not the first time I've had this dream."

A dream was different from a vision. "What was in this dream?"

"I saw my husband murdered. In our bed."

Ooh-kay. That was not what I expected. I worked hard not to judge. "Did you see who killed him?"

"No, I wasn't there when it happened."

"Just to be clear, your husband is still alive, right?" I'd had enough death for a while.

"Oh, yes."

"Do you think this dream means that your husband is in danger?" Had someone dumped something in the water supply that put people's lives on the line?

"I don't know. I was hoping you could help. You are a witch, right?"

"I am." I waited for her to tell me what she thought I could do though. Even Gertrude Poole, our most powerful witch in Witch's Cove, couldn't do much with a dream.

"I thought maybe you could do your sleuth thing and find out if there is anyone who wants to harm my Loughlin."

I had the sense it might be a long list. "What does your husband say about this?"

She planted a hand on her chest. "I haven't told him. He has enough stress in his life right now, what with trying to convince Mr. Hightower to sell."

"Perhaps if your husband was aware that his life was in danger, he might take some precaution."

"Maybe. I told Sheriff Rocker about it."

"That's good." I could only imagine his response. "What did he say?"

"That he couldn't do anything until someone actually tried to kill my husband. He recommended that I speak with you."

I was pleased that Steve hadn't totally dismissed me as a quack. "I can ask around for you."

"I'm willing to pay. I just want my husband safe."

The words *willing to pay* had my heart beating hard. "I understand."

"Who do you think would want to harm Mr. Merriman?" Jaxson asked. "We'll need a few names to look into. Such as who works with him? Or better yet, who his competitors are in town?"

"I can write down the names of his staff, but I don't know the workers. My son, Trevor, keeps track of that, but I can't imagine any of them wanting to harm Loughlin though. They all love him. As for competitors, we're basically the only developer who lives in Witch's Cove."

Our town only had a population of two thousand. While people always wanted homes, not many had new buildings built.

"I'm guessing your children wouldn't want to harm their father, right?" Jaxson asked.

He had investigated the family, so perhaps he knew something.

Mrs. Merriman's face turned to granite. "Absolutely not."

Since I hadn't heard what Jaxson had found out about Loughlin, I thought it would be best to learn what the wife had to say. "What are the names of your children, and do they live nearby?"

"I have three children, all of whom live in town. My oldest is Olivia. I will admit that she struggles a bit with her dad."

"Why is that?" I asked, trying to keep my voice soft and reassuring.

"She has a degree in civil engineering and an MBA, yet my husband thinks Trevor should run the company when Loughlin steps down."

She hadn't heard the father was ready to pass the torch. "He's planning to retire soon?" Didn't he want to build the condo?

"In the next year or two—after the new condos are built. Assuming they are. I also have twin sons, Trevor and DeWitt. They're twenty-seven. Even though DeWitt is a few minutes older, Loughlin wants Trevor to run the company. To our chagrin, he seems more interested in pursuing a career in art than building things. He was going to get an architectural degree, but he dropped out of school for some reason. Trevor works for our company, but I don't think his heart is in it."

"And DeWitt?" I asked. I remembered both of them from high school. Trevor was athletic, and while DeWitt was really smart, he didn't apply himself.

"DeWitt might be the brightest of the three, but his work ethic is, shall we say, lacking. He is too focused on how he thinks things should be done rather than finding out what the client really wants. It's why Loughlin wants Trevor to take over, though I have to admit DeWitt is an excellent marketer."

"Seems to me all three would be great at taking over," I said, not having any idea if that would even work.

"Agreed, but they don't see eye-to-eye on most issues. I suppose that's our fault."

Jaxson leaned forward. "How so?"

"My husband was always at work, and I probably spent more time on the tennis courts than I did at home raising the kids."

Sometimes wealth brought problems. "Do you think your husband would mind if we spoke to him?"

Her eyes widened. "Please don't say anything." She looked off to the side for a moment. "He thinks I'm a bit crazy as it is. I told him I was worried he was working too hard and that he should lose weight and exercise more, but he won't listen."

He seemed like a candidate for a heart attack more than Mr. Hightower. "Okay, we won't. You said he was under a lot of stress?"

"Yes, this new condo deal is driving him crazy."

"Was he particularly angry when Mr. Hightower refused to sell?" I wanted a second opinion.

"I'd say disappointed more than anything. Mr. Hightower's son was eager to sell, as was his daughter-in-law. We were hoping they could convince him. With Mr. Hightower's passing, I imagine things will go smoother."

The big question was whether anyone in the Merriman family helped the old man along to his grave?

## CHAPTER 5

Once Mrs. Merriman left, Jaxson and I worked on our murder board for about two hours, listing who might have wanted to kill Mr. Hightower and who might want to harm Mr. Merriman—assuming there was any credence to Divinity Merriman's psychic dream. She certainly seemed to think it had been real. And paying customers were always right.

My fingers were cramping from writing and erasing, and my brain was mush. "I say we call it quits for today. I'm sure Iggy is not happy that I left him home alone all day." Not that he couldn't leave and wander about whenever he wanted.

"You should bring him to the office tomorrow. I can feed him if you need to run around."

"That is so sweet of you. I would have suggested it for today, but Iggy told me he wanted to be around in case Sassy showed up."

Jaxson's lips turned into a smile. "He's dedicated like his mom."

"He is at that."

"While you see how our ghost whisperer is coming along,

I want to check out the Merriman kids. It would also be helpful to know the financial health of the company."

Jaxson was good at connecting the dots. "You want to see how important this condo construction is to his firm, I take it?"

He tapped my nose. "Give the witch a gold star—or rather a pink one."

I laughed. Jaxson had that effect on me. "We never got to have that lunch together. Maybe tomorrow?"

"Sure thing."

We had some leftover sandwiches in the fridge that he'd picked up from the convenience store, so I knew he wouldn't starve.

Curious to see if Iggy had learned anything, I hightailed it down the stairs, debating whether to sneak in through the beachside entrance so as not to be questioned by Aunt Fern or be brave and enter in the front. Since I really wanted to talk to Iggy, I chose the first plan, though I would fill Aunt Fern in on everything later.

At some point, I had to have a little get together with Penny, my best friend. The last two times I'd asked that we meet for a drink, she'd had a date with *her* hot guy, Hunter Ashwell, our resident forest ranger. I couldn't be happier that she'd finally found a man who not only treated her well, but he seemed to adore her seven-year old son.

I cleared my throat, not liking the trickle of envy that seemed to appear every time I thought about her happiness. Right now, I needed to focus on our first paying customer.

As I headed up the staircase, yelling sounded from my apartment. What the heck? I rushed inside to find Iggy on his stool looking down at Aimee, whose fur was sticking up. This wasn't good. At least I didn't detect any wounds on her. Iggy's claws, tail, and teeth could do some damage.

They both froze. "What's going on?" I asked.

"Iggy is cheating on me."

I didn't think it was my place to remind this cat that Iggy was an iguana, and the two of them were not compatible in that way. "Because he is trying to solve a murder case, and the only one who seems to know anything is a ghost?" I probably shouldn't have raised my voice, but I couldn't help it.

Aimee's fur went down. "Yes. I wouldn't have minded if he'd told me about her."

"Aimee, I asked Iggy not to fill you in right away."

"Why not?"

"Because I haven't told Aunt Fern what's happened yet. I wanted more information before I did." I didn't need her spreading rumors that weren't true.

"Did something happen?" Aimee asked, her tone sounding a little less shrill.

"Yes. Is Aunt Fern in her apartment?" Since I wasn't at work every day, I didn't know her schedule.

"No, but I can ask her to come up here if you want," Aimee offered.

It would be easier to tell everyone at once. "Okay."

As soon as Aimee left, I turned to Iggy. "What was that all about?"

He turned around. "I spoke with Sassy again, and I might have been gloating a little bit that I could see a ghost and Aimee couldn't."

So that was why his supposed girlfriend was mad. "That's not nice."

Iggy turned around. "I can see that now."

"Did Sassy give you any idea who might have harmed Mr. Hightower?"

"No. She did go back to the house to check that he was okay, however."

"Did she see me there?" I asked.

"Yes."

I wished I could have seen her. "If she could have appeared to me, I bet Mr. Hightower would have loved to have spoken to her."

I couldn't imagine what my life would be without Iggy. He was part of me.

"I'm the only lucky one, I guess." He puffed out his chest.

"Did she see Mr. Hightower grab his chest and collapse?" I still believed he'd been murdered.

"Sassy was roaming around the house, checking out where she used to sleep and stuff before she died. She heard a noise, but when she went to the living room, Mr. Hightower was on the floor. Dead."

"How terrible." Since ghosts didn't have bodies, it wasn't as if she could have called 9-1-1. "What did she do?"

"What could she do?"

"Good point."

The front door opened, and Aunt Fern came in, slightly out of breath. "Your mother told me you'd almost been arrested."

This was why I hadn't told her earlier. I didn't want her to be upset. "The sheriff wanted to ask me what I knew about Chester Hightower's death. That's all."

Aunt Fern sat on the sofa, and Aimee jumped up next to her. Probably because Iggy didn't like being number two, he climbed up next to my aunt and cuddled close.

"I'll start from the beginning." I went through my meeting with Mr. Hightower, about performing the spell, and then talking to the manager of the ice cream shop. "I then stopped by the sheriff's office to tell him what I knew. I had no idea that Mr. Hightower died right after I left."

"Are you sure the tea wasn't poisoned?" my aunt asked.

"He used store-bought teabags, and I had one too without any effects. Besides, until we get the autopsy report back—

assuming there is one—we can't be positive he didn't die of natural causes."

My aunt waved a dismissive hand. "Hogwash. Someone killed him. You said he looked to be in the pink of health. I mean, peak of health."

"I did." Though I imagine a lot of people felt and looked great minutes before their fatal heart attack, but what did I know?

"For now, let's assume it was murder," my aunt said.

"Okay, so who killed him?" I asked the motley crew of two animals and a human.

"Who had the most to gain by his death?" Aimee asked.

I almost did a double take. What did a cat know about motive? "Iggy, have you been regaling Aimee with sleuth stories?"

"They aren't stories. I like to tell her what really happened. You've solved a lot of crimes. I also told her about your spreadsheets."

Oh, boy. That would not endear Aimee to him. "Who had the most to gain, you ask? A lot of people." I went through the list, partially to catch them up, but also to see if maybe there were any flaws in what Jaxson and I had concluded this afternoon. "What do you all think?"

"I vote for Mrs. Merriman," Aimee said.

She hadn't been on my radar. "Why?"

"With Mr. Hightower dead, her husband could build the condo. That's more money for the family."

"It's possible. Anyone else?" I asked.

"I'm voting for Chester's daughter-in-law, Amanda," my aunt said.

"What's your reasoning?" Aunt Fern had an advantage over the others. She had her gossip queens at her disposal. By now, I bet she'd contacted each one—maybe more than once.

"I heard she's broke."

"Mr. Hightower said she lived above her means, but why kill him? He probably would have passed away within a few years anyway. I imagine both she and Darren would inherit everything." That would be something to ask a lawyer—or Steve.

"She needs the money now. I think she gambles," my aunt said.

"Who told you that?"

Aunt Fern shrugged. "I don't kiss and tell."

Maybe that was what Mr. Hightower meant by bad investments. "And detective Iggy? What's your take?"

"My money is on the butler."

I had to laugh. "There's a butler?"

"The butler always does it. I've been watching a lot of mystery television shows."

Now he was just showing off. "Let's stick to the list of suspects."

"Fine. I pick DeWitt Merriman."

He wasn't on my radar either. "Why?"

"He wants his dad to succeed so he can prove to him that he should take over the business. If Mr. Hightower is dead, then his dad will need help building this new condo. It can be his chance to shine."

"I'm not sure he has the drive to do something like that." I held up a hand. "But you could be right."

"I'm sure you, or our wonderful sheriff's department, will find the killer soon," Aunt Fern said.

"I hope so. When we figure out who it is, we will toast the winner." I smiled.

"Wait. You haven't given us your choice," Iggy said.

"I don't have a favorite."

"You must be leaning toward someone," he said.

I didn't want to pick anyone who'd been chosen. "What about Loughlin Merriman? He has the most to gain, I guess."

Aunt Fern shook her head. "He would have paid someone to do it. I don't think Merriman is the type to get his hands dirty."

"Where did you hear that?"

"People talk."

That was good information.

Once I'd filled everyone in regarding the rest of what I knew, Aimee and my aunt headed across the hall to their apartment.

It was time to scrounge up some food before heading to bed. If Jaxson and I were to investigate who wanted to harm Mr. Merriman, we had a lot of people to talk to tomorrow.

Just as I was about to put something in the microwave, a sharp rap sounded on my door. It wasn't Jaxson. I knew his knock.

Not sure who to expect, I looked through the peephole. A band tightened around my chest as I yanked open the door. "Sheriff? Is something wrong?"

That was a stupid question. Of course, something was wrong, or he wouldn't be there.

"I'm sorry to bother you, but I've arrested Mrs. Divinity Merriman for the murder."

My mind spun. "You think *she* killed Mr. Hightower?" If that turned out to be true, Aimee would be impossible to be around.

"What? No. She murdered her husband."

"Loughlin Merriman is dead?" I was having a hard time keeping up with people keeling over.

"Yes. In fact, it was Mrs. Merriman who reported his death."

"Yet you suspect her?"

"She had blood all over her when we arrived."

"That doesn't prove she killed him. Did Mrs. Merriman tell you she'd asked me to look into her psychic vision?"

"She did."

"I assume she's called her lawyer?"

"She has," he said.

What was up with all of the short answers. "Are you asking me to investigate?"

I swore his lips almost turned up. "No, Glinda. I want to know what she told you."

"Come in. I'm not sure I can be very helpful though."

"You never know."

I would have offered him a drink, but he'd always turned me down in the past. He slipped onto the chair, so I took the sofa. No surprise, Iggy scurried over and crawled up next to me. Too bad the sheriff couldn't hear what my familiar had to say.

"Tell me about Mrs. Merriman's dream."

"She told you all ready."

He nodded. "Yes, but she might have filled in a few things when she retold it to you."

"Just that she'd had this vision a few times. Each one had her finding her husband dead in their bed."

"His bed?"

"Yes. Why? Where did he die?"

"He was murdered in his office."

"You're certain it wasn't a heart attack? Mrs. Merriman said he was under a lot of stress." I waved a hand. "Never mind. You said she had blood on her hands. Was he shot?"

"Actually, he was hit on the back of his head with a heavy object. We think it might have been an award Mr. Merriman had."

"And you dusted for fingerprints?"

He huffed. "Of course. The only prints I found belonged to Mrs. Merriman though."

That wasn't good. "And not the deceased? His would be there. It was his award."

Steve dragged a hand down his mouth. "You're right, but the only ones we found belonged to the wife. That is interesting."

Pride filled me. "That implies the person who wielded the fatal blow wore gloves."

"You might be onto something."

## CHAPTER 6

"Will you release Mrs. Merriman?" I asked the sheriff. Surely, he would after my brilliant observation about the lack of fingerprints other than my client's.

"Not yet. How about stopping over tomorrow and talking with her? She might be more willing to chat with you. It's possible, she'll slip up about what happened in that office."

He wanted her to be guilty. I didn't like that, but at least I'd planted a seed of doubt in his mind. "I'll be happy to, or would you rather I go now?" I was about to eat and then head to bed, but I could put that off for a bit.

"No. It's late, and even I need my sleep."

And here I thought Steve Rocker was a super hero who never slept. "Works for me."

As soon as I showed him out, I called Jaxson.

"Hey," he said.

"You won't believe what happened."

"Mr. Merriman is dead."

Really? "How did you find out so fast?"

"Drake told me."

"Drake? How did he hear?" Why wasn't anything making sense to me?

"Don't you remember? Drake and Trevor became friends when they were on the same high school baseball team."

"I didn't know they kept in touch."

"They grab a drink every now and then."

"If they were mere acquaintances, why call Drake?"

"Because his mom hired The Pink Iguana Sleuths to help her."

Of course. "That makes sense. Did Trevor offer any insight into his dad's death?"

"Not really. He's still in shock that his father is dead and that his mother is accused of the crime. He isn't buying it though. His mom was flighty but not vindictive. All she seemed to care about was playing tennis and shopping."

"I can't imagine what Trevor is going through." I physically shivered. "I called to tell you that, but also to say Steve personally stopped over to tell me about the death, because Mrs. Merriman is our client. He asked if I'd speak with her tomorrow."

"Interesting. Are you going to see her?"

"Sure. He thinks she'll relate more to a woman."

"That's probably true."

I couldn't tell if he wanted me to invite him or not. "I'll stop over as soon as I finish with her. I'm sure you have your hands full with Drake. He must be upset too."

"He is a bit."

I yawned. "It's late. I'm going to try to get some shut eye."

"You do that. Night, pink lady."

"Night."

After I put out some greens and fresh water for Iggy, I microwaved something to eat and then readied for bed. No surprise, my mind refused to stop spinning. Sure, Divinity would be covered in blood if she found her husband, but if she'd killed him, wouldn't she have changed and then let someone else find him—like one of her children?

As hard as I tried to put Mr. Hightower's and Mr. Merriman's death out of my mind, I couldn't. By the time the sun came up, I was done trying to sleep. I decided to eat breakfast downstairs instead of making something myself, because I wanted to be surrounded by happy people.

"Glinda," Aunt Fern said. "What are you doing up so early?"

I'd spent three years working the morning shift, so she shouldn't be that surprised. "I couldn't sleep."

"I guess you heard about Mr. Merriman."

This was ridiculous. Had I been the last person to learn of his death? "Yes, the sheriff stopped by to tell me my client had been arrested. Isn't that great? Our first paying customer, and she lands in jail."

"All the more reason to find out who really did it."

That was the first good piece of advice I'd heard in a while. "Thank you. I'm going to have some breakfast for a change and then talk to Mrs. Merriman."

"Smart."

My aunt motioned for me to sit at one of Penny's tables. We weren't busy so she had time to sit and talk. "Hey, stranger," she said. "This is a nice surprise."

I explained that we finally had our first client, but that now she was in jail, accused of murder. "I have my work cut out for me."

"I can see that." Penny placed a hand on mine. "I miss our chats."

It wasn't as if I hadn't suggested we get together a few times. "I do too. We have to make a date."

She smiled. "I know. How about you, me, Hunter, and Jaxson grab a bite sometime?"

"I'm not dating Jaxson."

"I know, but why not give it a shot? I know you think he's hot."

"He's too valuable as a partner. If we dated, and I messed it up, he'd quit. Then The Pink Iguana Sleuths would fall apart. I need him."

"Then don't mess it up. How do you think he feels about you?"

"You know I'm terrible at judging a man's interest."

Penny nodded. "I know. Okay maybe we can go to the movies. Then you wouldn't have to talk."

"I'm not even sure the theater is open, what with Darren mourning his father's death. Besides, we can't catch up when we're in the theater."

My friend sucked in a breath. "There is that. This town is getting scary. We just get the werewolf deaths under control, and then people start killing each other."

"I think having a beast tearing you limb from limb is worse, despite the outcome being the same."

"Probably true." Three more parties came in, and Penny stood. "What do you want to eat?"

"A coffee and a number three special." I didn't have to look at the menu. I'd memorized it.

"Coming right up."

My life certainly had gone out of control fast. I loved trying to solve crimes, but I hadn't spent much time of late with Iggy or my aunt. I should be happy that Penny seemed to be consumed with Hunter Ashwell, or I'd be ditching her, too, for my new non-paying job.

Once my meal arrived, I scarfed it down. I hadn't realized how hungry I was. While I ate, I tried to figure out what questions to ask Divinity Merriman. I couldn't imagine what it would be like to be in jail while grieving for a husband.

After I finished, I said goodbye to Penny and my aunt, with a promise to catch up with them when I had the chance.

I crossed the street and entered the sheriff's department. This time when Pearl looked up, she smiled, and then shoved a plateful of cookies my way. "I'm sorry."

"For what?" I asked.

"For the way I treated you."

"I don't understand."

"Oh, Glinda. When Steve and Nash said they needed to talk to you about Chester Hightower's murder, I assumed they were going to arrest you. I never should have thought that."

She was sweet. "It's understandable. I was the last person to see him alive—other than the killer—assuming he was murdered, that is. Anyhoo, Steve asked that I speak with my client, Mrs. Merriman."

"That poor woman."

Why didn't Pearl think she was guilty? I mentally waved a hand. "Is the sheriff or the deputy in?

"I thought I heard your voice," Steve said as he rounded the corner, probably coming from his office.

"Sheriff, I'd like to see Mrs. Merriman."

"Of course." He motioned I follow him to the conference room. "Wait here while I get her."

I passed on the cookies for now and trailed after him. I was thankful he didn't ask me to sit in some nasty cell to speak with her. A minute later, a rather haggard looking woman walked in. At least she had on clean clothes—orange though they may be.

When she saw me, her eyes brightened. "Glinda, I'm so happy to see a friendly face."

That probably meant I should smile. "How are you holding up?"

"I've never been in jail. I miss everything."

I imagine she missed her makeup, her comb, brush, and other toiletries. "Are they treating you okay?"

"Oh, yes, but it's like I'm in a dream."

A dream was what got her into trouble in the first place. "Can you walk me through what happened?"

"Sure." She inhaled. "When Loughlin didn't call or come home for dinner, I went to the office. To be honest, I thought maybe he was having an affair."

Whoa. I hadn't even considered that. And why hadn't she mentioned that before? "With whom?"

"I don't know, but the late nights and secretive phone calls led me to think that."

That was something I'd have to ask Steve about. "What happened next?"

She shook her head. "It's all a blur. When I entered my husband's office, I found him face down on the floor. At first, I thought he'd fainted. He has low blood pressure, and when he stands up too fast, he whites out."

"Whites out?"

"Gets light headed. He has to stop until the episode passes. Only then did I see the blood and the big gash on the back of his head." Tears streamed down her face. It was hard for me to watch her relive her worst nightmare. "Next to him was that award he'd been given for best contractor. It had blood on it."

"Did you touch the award?"

She nodded. "I wasn't sure if Loughlin was dead, so I wanted to roll him over, only the award was in the way. I had to move it to the side."

Everything she said made sense. I had no idea how much blood she had on her, but if that had been my husband or a loved one, I would have cradled him in my arms. "Did you hold him?"

She choked and nodded.

"Who do you think did this?"

"I...don't...know."

Her mind probably wasn't focused on solving the mystery but rather on her loss. I turned toward the glass wall where Steve was watching us. I waved for him to come in.

"Thank you, Mrs. Merriman. I will do everything I can to find out who did this."

She looked up with her tear-streaked face. "Thank you."

Steve told me to wait in his office while he escorted Mrs. Merriman back to her cell. That poor woman. While I was no expert, I'd spent the last three years dealing with people at the restaurant, and while Mrs. Merriman wasn't perfect, I didn't peg her as a murderer.

Pearl was on the phone when I slipped out of the soundproof room to Steve's office. A moment later, Steve and Nash came in. Were they both dying to hear my opinion? Somehow, I didn't think so.

"I'd like your take on what she told you," Steve said.

"I don't think she did it."

"Why is that?" he asked.

"Her actions were consistent with a grieving spouse. She explained how the blood got on her and how her fingerprints were on the murder weapon—assuming that's what caused the fatal blow."

"I watched her the whole time. While I couldn't hear the conversation, she appeared sincere," Steve said.

"And did you see the sorrow on her face. I don't think she's faking it." I leaned forward. "I know you said her fingerprints were on the award, but where? If I were to kill someone with a glass award, I would pick it up by the base. Is that where you found her prints?" I didn't let him answer before continuing. "For power, I would think she'd use both hands. Did you find all ten prints?"

My heart was actually racing.

Nash placed a hand on my arm. He seemed to be assigned

the role of calming me down should I get out of control. "We considered that."

Oh. "And?"

Neither answered.

"On a different note," Steve said. "I'd like you to take a look at another crime scene." He pulled out an eight by ten photo and handed it to me.

"This is Mr. Hightower's kitchen. Are you saying his heart attack wasn't from natural causes?" It would be the only reason he'd be investigating.

"I am. We received the autopsy back this morning. He died of a heart attack all right, but he had no blocked arteries, and his heart looked healthy. Dr. Sanchez believes something caused it to stop."

"Like what? Poison?" I couldn't think of anything else. Oleander leaves had killed the former deputy.

"The good doctor is doing some testing. She is testing the stomach content to see if something in there was the issue. As a double check, both of us thought perhaps you'd like to have a go at it."

It took a moment for me to realize he was asking me to use my gemstone to determine cause of death. "I can try, but the best I'll be able to do is confirm it was poison, not what kind."

"Or you might find something else."

"You have a point."

Steve nodded to the picture. "Is this how you remember the scene when you left Mr. Hightower—alive."

I studied it. "No. We used white porcelain cups that had pink and green flowers on them. We most certainly didn't use yellow ceramic mugs."

"We didn't see any cups in the sink."

"That's because I put them in a near empty dishwasher.

They should still be there. I hope you collected the coffee cups. Maybe that's how the poison was delivered."

It looked as if both Steve and Nash were fighting a smile. "We did. Our lab is testing them now, though I doubt a killer would be so careless as to leave evidence like that."

"Maybe it's a poison that doesn't leave a trace."

Steve's brows pinched. "Such as?"

"I don't know." But with a little bit of research, I bet I could narrow it down. "I'll try to find out."

"Good. Thank you, Glinda," Steve said.

"You're welcome. Oh, did Dr. Sanchez find any puncture wounds by any chance?"

"No, and trust me, she checked. After the last fiasco with Deputy Duncan, she looked very carefully."

That would take any poison that needed to be injected off the table. Good to know. "What's going to happen to Mrs. Merriman?"

"We'll study the evidence again. If we find we don't have enough, we'll let her go. That doesn't mean we can't arrest her later if we find something definitive."

"That's fair, though I'm sure you'll find nothing. I don't think she is guilty." That meant it was up to me and Jaxson to help look for the real killer. The problem was that I had also promised Iggy I would try to find out who killed Mr. Hightower. No one else better die, or I might hang up my shingle.

"We'll see."

## CHAPTER 7

As soon as I left the sheriff's office, I realized I should have asked when my mother would be receiving Mr. Hightower's body, but it didn't really matter. It was easy enough to check. I called her.

"Glinda. This is a nice surprise."

I was so happy she sounded like herself again. Phone calls from her sister were always hard, but I didn't like that she acted as if I never spoke to her. I visited her yesterday!

"I just came from the sheriff's office, and he—"

"Oh, no. Were you arrested again? Is this your one phone call?"

My mother usually wasn't this anxious. "Nothing like that." I explained that Steve asked me to see if I could detect the cause of Mr. Hightower's death.

"That's wonderful, sweetie. I'll be receiving him in a bit."

"Great. I'll change and be right over." My clothes often smelled after doing one of these analysis, and I would rather not get the ones I was wearing stinky.

Once I disconnected, I rushed home. As soon as I stepped

inside, Iggy raced up to my feet. "Hey, buddy. Did you sleuth today?"

His stomach dropped onto the floor. "No. I couldn't find Sassy again."

"I'm sorry. I'm sure if she learns anything, she'll show up. If she does, could you ask her something for me?"

He lifted his head. "What is it?"

"If Sassy was in the house when Mr. Hightower was murdered—"

"He was murdered?"

I needed to fill him in. "Yes. Dr. Sanchez did the autopsy. She thinks he might have been poisoned." Okay, I drew that conclusion. "She even asked that I try my pink crystal discovery process on the body."

"Can I come?"

"To the mortuary?"

"Yes."

"When I took you to the bowling alley, you almost gagged on the smell of lane oil," I said.

"I'll be good. I promise. Maybe I can get Aunt Fern to make me a mask for the next time."

I laughed. "Maybe."

His energy level jumped up a notch. "What should I ask Sassy if I see her?"

"Ask her if she smelled anything in the house before Mr. Hightower died."

"Like what?"

"Like a woman's perfume, a man's cologne, or perhaps pipe smoke. Everyone has an odor."

Iggy swished his tail. "I don't smell."

"Maybe not." Though he'd never washed with soap despite his love of water. "I need to change. I'll be right out."

Once I tossed on some grubby clothes, I went back into the living room. "Ready to be grossed out?"

"I am made of sterner stuff than that."

We'll see. "You are."

I had a feeling he believed that if he went to a place where there were dead people that he might be able to contact Sassy. I had to admit it had merit, assuming his thought process was that good. Iggy was only fifteen years old—and teenagers weren't known for clear thinking—especially boys.

I placed him in my purse and off we went. Once we reached the funeral home, I entered through the back entrance where I found my mom in the embalming room with the body.

"Mr. Hightower just arrived."

"I can see that."

"Would you like me to stay while you do your magic?"

"If you have work to do, I understand, but I can always use a second opinion."

Mom smiled. "I'll stay."

"Good."

Just like I had done many times before, I removed my magical necklace from around my neck and began at Mr. Hightower's feet. I didn't want to presume that the gem would turn purple when it reached his stomach. That color would have implied the man had been poisoned. Unfortunately, poison was fickle. If it didn't stay long in his body, I'd detect nothing.

With care, I moved my gem back and forth, closely monitoring the color of the gem. As I reached his stomach, I hovered the stone close to the body.

"There," my mother said. "I thought I saw it change to purple."

She might be more unbiased than me. "It did, but only for a moment."

Next, I headed up to the heart, but once more I didn't

detect anything of significance. That was very strange. "If my gem is right, this man should be alive."

"Glinda, please."

"Okay, okay. I believe he was poisoned, but there isn't much of it left in his system. Dr. Sanchez is doing some testing, so hopefully, she'll learn something. I agree that he was helped along with his heart attack."

"That's a start, I guess."

"I wish it were more," I said.

I was a bit dejected that I couldn't add much to the doctor's diagnosis. After repeating the procedure once more, I drew the same conclusion, which was that he might have been poisoned. Unfortunately, that didn't help me or the sheriff find the killer. I could only hope there was something in his house that would give him a clue.

Iggy poked his head out of my purse. "That was a bust, wasn't it?"

I'd honestly forgotten he was there. "I guess, but I'm not going to make up something just to impress our sheriff."

"Fine. How about we get out of here then?"

I chuckled. The smell had been too much for him, as I suspected. "Sure." I turned to my mother. "Do you think you can try to contact our deceased?"

"I can try, but it usually takes them a while before they are ready to talk."

She always said that, but just this once, I was hoping we'd have a chatty corpse. "Thanks. Iggy and I are off to see what Jaxson can dig up."

She hugged me goodbye and then patted Iggy on the head. "You be good."

"When am I not good?"

Mom laughed. Iggy and I left, and I was happy to be out in the fresh air. Iggy poked his head out of my purse again and crawled up my arm onto my shoulder. "Who are we going to interview next?"

"I want to bring Jaxson up to speed now that we need to put Mr. Hightower's death back on the table."

"Good. Assuming I ever see Sassy again. I don't want to disappoint her."

I looked down at him. "Is there something going on between you two?"

"No, but she's a friend."

My poor familiar. I never realized he was so lonely. Once at the Wine and Cheese Emporium, I climbed the stairs to our office. To my delight, Jaxson was there.

"Hey."

He spun around. "You look...casual."

"Uh oh. I'm sorry. I was analyzing Mr. Hightower's body. I should have changed."

"Perfect timing." He stood, disappeared to the back, and then returned. "I'm glad Iggy is here. I have a present for each of you."

I never expected that. "What is it?"

He plucked Iggy off my shoulder. "I think you are going to like this, young man." He removed Iggy's pink rhinestone collar.

"What are you doing?" I asked, trying to keep the slight panic out of my voice.

"I think it is time our associate here gets something a bit more dignified than a pink bow." From behind his back, Jaxson produced a black leather collar.

"Wow. I love it," Iggy said. "What does the metal piece say?"

"You read it," Jaxson said.

"Detective Iggy." My very happy familiar turned around to face me. "I'm glad someone understands me."

He was right. I should have replaced his collar a long time

ago, but a black collar? "I think it's awesome, too. Thank you, Jaxson."

"Ditto," Iggy said. "Put it on me. Please?"

Jaxson obliged. I had to admit, Iggy looked good. "You are the best looking iguana in the world," I announced.

Iggy lifted up his head. "Where's a mirror?"

Jaxson carried him to the back room. Their male bonding moment was cute. When Jaxson returned with Iggy, Jaxson was wearing a different T-shirt.

"That's new," I said.

He smiled. "I thought we all could use a pick me up." He handed me a light pink T-shirt. On the front, in dark pink letters, it said Pink Iguana Sleuths. In the corner was our logo—a pink iguana. "That is so cute."

His was the same, except his shirt was black with pink letters. "We're ready to be professionals," he announced as he lifted his chin in pride.

It would take more than a new shirt, but I loved it anyway. Having Jaxson as my partner had been one of my best decisions.

I dropped down onto the sofa. "I've had a busy morning."

I regaled them with my visit to the jail to speak with our client, Mrs. Merriman, and then how Steve told me that Mr. Hightower's death had been elevated to murder.

"I was right!" Iggy said. "Or rather Sassy was right."

"Yes, you were. I did my crystal analysis and only noticed a trace of poison. I'm hoping that the lab can figure out what kind it was."

"Should we focus our efforts on Mr. Hightower's murder or the murder of Loughlin Merriman?" Jaxson asked.

"If we have to choose, I think we should concentrate on Mr. Merriman. His wife doesn't need to stay in jail any longer than necessary."

Iggy was still perched on Jaxson's shoulder. He seemed to have found his new hero.

Footsteps sounded from the inside stairwell. A moment later Drake appeared. "Hey, you two."

He wasn't his usual chipper self, but I could understand since his friend was so distraught. "How's Trevor holding up?" I asked.

"He's upset, and who can blame him? He's basically lost both of his parents and his livelihood."

"I thought his father was going to step down and put him in charge. Trevor can run the company as planned."

"Yes, but he isn't really interested in the business. Out of respect for his dad, he agreed to take over. With his father gone, he wants to go back to school. The problem is that the money to pay for it will be tied up in the courts until this murder investigation is finished."

"What can we do?" his brother asked.

"Find out who killed Loughlin."

"Trevor still has no idea who wanted his father dead?"

Drake slid onto the sofa and faced me. "I had to drag it out of him, but now that the shock has kind of worn off, he kind of thinks it might have been his sister, Olivia."

"Whoa. Why?"

"She's never gotten along with her dad. He treats her like she has no worth, but she's the most talented of the three kids."

"That's no reason to kill him."

Drake shrugged. "Trevor has no proof, other than she said she was going to have a heart-to-heart with dear old dad yesterday about the way he treated her. She was planning on quitting if he didn't change his ways." Drake held up his hand. "Trevor said if Olivia was the culprit, it wasn't premeditated. She was on medication for her anger but often forgets to take her pills."

Intriguing. "Being treated less than equal would rub me the wrong way, too." I was lucky that I was an only child.

"So, you'll help?" Drake asked.

"Of course," Jaxson and I said in unison. I inwardly smiled at how alike our minds often were.

"While you two figure out how to solve Mr. Merriman's murder, I'm heading over to the bookstore to buy a book on poisons," I said. "We need some good reference material."

"Good," Jaxson said. "But don't be upset if my brother and I solve the case while you're gone."

I had to laugh. "Go for it. Don't forget you're in charge of Iggy."

Jaxson saluted.

I took the outside staircase and headed south toward the bookstore. The walk would give me time to think. If only the ghost of Mr. Merriman would appear and tell me who killed him, this case solving stuff would be so much easier. Not that I expected a ghost to jump out at me, but I could hope.

For a weekday, the bookstore was fairly crowded, which surprised me. However, it would give me time to look around without Betty hovering. The reference materials were easy to find. To my delight, Betty and Frank Sanchez actually had a few books that would suit my needs perfectly, but it made me wonder why this small store would have several books on poison.

The contents of the book I picked ranged from poisonous household products to poisonous plants, deadly animals—like snakes and spiders—to medical and industrial poisons. For sure, it would provide a killer with a lot of knowledge.

"Glinda," Betty said behind my back, startling me.

"Hey, I'm just looking for a good book on poison." Since I had one in my hand, she could probably deduce that.

Her eyes widened. "Are you planning to kill someone?"

I laughed. "Why would you ask that?"

Betty patted me on the back. "Only kidding." She pulled a different book off the shelf. "This is my best seller."

I didn't want to think that a lot of people were plotting murders. "Best seller? Anyone buy one recently?"

She looked around and then leaned close. "You won't believe this, but Amanda Hightower did a few days ago. Said she wanted to get rid of some rats that had infested the theater."

"That makes sense. The place is old." Though I didn't picture Mrs. Amanda Hightower doing rodent control. That would be something Darren would take care of—or a pest control company.

"I'll take that book then."

"Anything else I can help you with?"

Betty was always good for some gossip. "I'm guessing you heard that Loughlin Merriman was murdered in his office yesterday."

"I did. How terrible."

"Drake is a friend of the family, and I promised him I'd ask around." That sounded better than saying our firm was representing the murder suspect. "Any idea who might have wanted to harm him?"

"I had no real interaction with the man, but rumor has it that Samantha Darling and he were *close*." She wiggled her eyebrows, implying they were having an affair. This meshed with what Mrs. Merriman mentioned.

I, however, didn't see those two together. Samantha, while pretty, didn't seem the rich man's type. "I appreciate the intel. Have you heard any dirt on Olivia, his daughter?"

Betty dipped her head, clearly trying to remember more gossip. "Just that she's a very private person. I don't think she's very outgoing. She works for her dad all the time."

"Good to know."

I paid for my book and then had to stop at the sheriff's

department to give him the news about how Mr. Hightower might have died.

When I entered the office, Pearl wasn't there. Jennifer Larson, who usually worked nights was manning the desk, but I didn't want to ask about the sudden shift change. "Is the sheriff in?"

"What is this about?"

"Mr. Hightower's death."

"One moment."

Steve came out of the back a few seconds later and motioned me toward his office. Instead of sitting at his desk, we sat across from each other.

"What did you find out?" he asked.

## CHAPTER 8

"I'm as confused about Mr. Hightower's death as Dr. Sanchez is," I said. That wasn't what Steve wanted to hear, but it was the truth.

"Do you think he died of natural causes?" Steve asked.

"No." I explained that I spotted a quick flash of color to indicate poison. "The curious part was that I detected no discernible issues with his heart."

"Interesting."

"Did Dr. Sanchez learn anything else about his condition?"

"Not yet, but she's waiting on the lab results before she writes her final report."

From the way he wasn't meeting my gaze, I didn't think he was telling me the whole truth. From my purse, I pulled out the new book I'd purchased. "This is a book on poisons."

"Glinda."

I disliked that tone. "It's for future cases too, but here's the interesting part. Guess who also bought this book a few days ago?"

"Joan of Arc, Attila the Hun, or Son of Sam?"

"Funny. It was Amanda Hightower."

His chin dipped. "That is intriguing. Do you have any insight as to what she planned to use the book for?"

"She claimed there were rats in the theater. While it's possible, I don't see her personally getting rid of them. I know money is tight for Darren, but come on, how much does an exterminator cost?"

He stood, went around his desk, and pulled out his yellow pad. The man needed to invest in some sort of electronic tablet to make his life simpler. He jotted down something. "I'll look into it."

That worked for me. I wasn't into rodent killing anyway. "According to Betty, the owner of the Candles Bookstore, she heard that Mr. Merriman was having an affair with Samantha Darling."

"Really? Why is that?"

Why? I thought affairs were obvious. They found each other attractive. "I don't know the details."

"I'm sure you are aware that Samantha manages the Beachside Condos, a development built by Loughlin Merriman. Perhaps, he was just checking up on her."

Steve had a way of poking holes through a lot of my theories. "Could be."

"Any other gossip imparted by our bookstore owner?"

He didn't have to sound so smug. "I asked if maybe Olivia was seeing anyone, but she said Merriman's daughter seemed to be all work and no play."

"I see. So, no additional suspects?"

I debated whether to mention what Trevor told Drake. Why not? I hadn't been sworn to secrecy, and I would like it if Trevor got closure for his father's death. "Trevor suspects Olivia might be the killer."

"Seriously? Did he say why?" That finally got his attention.

I went through his logic about how their dad didn't respect her, even though she was the most qualified to run the business. "It was the same thing that Mrs. Merriman said about her."

"Nash is investigating Olivia's alibi right now."

Oh. "Okay."

"Thank you, Glinda. You've been helpful."

I didn't see how, but why debate it? With nothing else to reveal, I headed back to the office. When I arrived, Iggy was running around, jumping on the furniture, acting as if he owned the place. "You look excited," I said to my familiar.

"I'm practicing my victory dance for when we find the killer."

"Or killers," I corrected.

"Yes. Aimee will be so jealous."

Everything always seemed to come down to that cat. "I hope she appreciates you."

Jaxson turned around. "Did you find the book on poison that you were looking for?"

"I did. I also learned some interesting facts." I pulled the book from my backpack and handed it to him.

Jaxson leafed through it. "This is dangerous. Who knew that Lily of the Valley was poisonous? My mother loved that plant."

"Right? And Star of Bethlehem. I'm glad it's not grown around here, because it causes shortness of breath and death."

Jaxson whistled. "I wonder if anyone else has seen this book."

I smiled. "Betty told me Amanda Hightower bought that book a few days ago."

"Did you tell Steve?"

"I did. I will have to admit, he and Nash seem to be on top of things."

"But I'm betting you'll want to interview her, right?"

I shook my head. "Not really. I think we have a better chance of learning stuff by talking to the gossipers. Did you find out if Merriman Developers was hurting financially?"

"Nothing pointed to that fact. Mr. Hightower, however, had taken out a few loans in the last two years, probably to keep the theater afloat."

"He said he was losing money, but I didn't know it was to the point where he'd need a loan. How did you learn about that? You've always said you're against hacking into bank records."

Jaxson smiled. "My information came from a source."

Good to know Jaxson was making connections in this town. "Speaking of sources, in theory, Loughlin Merriman was having an affair with Samantha Darling."

"Who is she?"

"She is the manager of the Beachside Condos, the ones that were developed by Merriman's company."

"I think that is where Trevor Merriman lives."

"That would make sense. He probably gets free rent. Maybe he's the one who is having the affair and not his father."

Jaxson chuckled. "At this point, anything is possible. I think I'll bring our suspect board out here where we can work on it. I figure we'll need to add a few more people."

"Like Samantha Darling?"

"Why not? Loughlin Merriman might have wanted to hand over the company to Trevor so he could ride off in the sunset with his new honey."

"Then why kill Mr. Merriman?"

Jaxson shrugged. "He might have changed his mind. Maybe he decided to stay with his wife, and Samantha was banking on sharing Loughlin's money."

"That theory has potential, but why not kill the wife instead?"

"Good point."

"How about putting on your sleuthing hat and see what you can learn from her? I bet you can tell if the woman is grieving or not."

"Sure. What will you be doing in the meantime?"

He probably wanted to make certain I wasn't planning to do anything stupid. "Looking over the poison book. While I'd love to talk to Olivia, Nash has already grilled her."

"If she is the killer, I don't want you anywhere near her."

He was right. Before Jaxson could even stand up, someone knocked on our door. It opened, and my aunt entered. I never expected to see her here, even though the Tiki Hut Grill was only two doors away. "Aunt Fern, is everything okay?"

A little out of breath, she wiped her brow. "Those are a lot of steps. It doesn't help that it's hot out there."

Jaxson jumped up. "Can I get you a cold bottle of water?"

"Would you?" She walked over to the sofa and dropped down. Iggy rushed over and climbed onto her lap. "Hey there, champ." Aunt Fern lifted Iggy's collar. "Where did you get this?"

"Jaxson got it for me. It has my new title on it. I wish Glinda had thought of it years ago."

He was never going to let me live that down. "Well, you have it now."

Jaxson returned and handed my aunt the cold drink. Naturally, he'd already removed the cap. The man was almost too perfect, which only proved that I couldn't date him since I couldn't afford to lose him.

"What brings you here, Aunt Fern?" I asked.

"Gossip. What else?"

I loved gossip. Both Jaxson and I sat across from her. "Do

tell."

"Well, Nash and Dr. Sanchez came into the Tiki Hut for some lunch."

"Did you seat them near the condiment table so you could pretend to be filling up the ketchup, mustard, and salt and pepper shakers in order to overhear their conversation?" I asked.

Truth be told, I had learned a lot that way.

"It doesn't matter my method." She clasped her hands together. I know that meant I'd have to work to get her to talk.

"I'm sorry. Please tell us."

"Very well. Dr. Sanchez learned that Mr. Hightower's trousers had traces of Barbados nut shells sprinkled on them."

"I don't understand. Did he have them as part of his last meal or something?"

"Yes, and apparently these nuts are poisonous."

My mind spun. "Do you think he ate these nuts and had an allergic reaction?"

"I'm no doctor, but from the way Dr. Sanchez was smiling, she seemed to think this was the key to how he died."

"Are you saying he died from natural causes then? That no one helped him along?"

"Not necessarily," Jaxson said. "Most people know what they are allergic to, and nut allergies are huge." He stood, walked over to his desk, and retrieved the poison book. It only took him a minute to find something. "It says here the Barbados tree grows in warm climates, including Florida."

"Good to know, but does it cause your heart to stop or something?" I asked.

"Not exactly, but it causes difficulty breathing. I bet if you're in your eighties, it might kill you."

"I imagine Dr. Sanchez would have found out. Good

sleuthing, Aunt Fern."

She smiled. "Thank you. This means he was murdered, right?"

"It's certainly possible. We'll go with that until it is ruled otherwise."

We chatted a bit more, and once my Aunt left, Jaxson took off for his first solo assignment—interviewing Samantha Darling. Like Divinity Merriman, Samantha was a beautiful woman. Only Samantha was twenty years younger than Loughlin's wife. I refused to be jealous that Jaxson would be interviewing her. I trusted him.

While I waited for him to return, I checked out our board again. Each suspect had a sticky note and on it was pertinent information related to the case. I'd already added two things about Amanda Hightower. One, that she was a gambler who was broke. That was consistent with the living-above-her-means profile that Mr. Hightower had mentioned. People should only gamble what they could afford to lose—unless they were desperate, I guess. Secondly, she'd be aware if her father-in-law was allergic to nuts. But if he were, he'd know it and wouldn't eat them. Ugh. Why did everything have to be so complicated?

Next, I created a note for Samantha Darling. The only way she'd be angry enough to harm Mr. Merriman was if he tried to break up with her. I also had sticky notes for all three of Mr. Merriman's children. Olivia planned to stop by her father's office right before he died, and she had motive. DeWitt might have wanted to inherit the business and been angry because their father chose Trevor over him. As the eldest twin, he might have thought it was his right to be next in line. Besides, he knew his brother didn't want the responsibility. It's possible DeWitt had gone to his dear old dad's office to convince him of that fact and a heated argument ensued. The same could be said for Trevor, too. He wanted to go back to school, and he might have believed that the only way to achieve his goal was to kill his father. The problem with that logic was that the money would be tied up until after the legal proceedings.

To be fair to all, I had to add something to Divinity's note. I wrote that she could have confronted her husband about the affair. He might have told her he wanted out of the marriage, and that might have been something she'd never be able to live with. Out of rage, she picked up the award and bashed him over the head, and then pretended to come in and find him dead. That sounded just as feasible as the other scenarios.

So far, no one mentioned any of his workers holding a grudge against the boss. If I knew any of their names, I would ask them directly. But wait. Trevor knew who they were, and I bet Drake could get the list from his good friend.

"Iggy, I'm going downstairs to talk to Drake. Do you want to come or wait up here?"

"I'll stay."

That was almost too easy and perhaps unwise on my part to leave him. Most likely, he wanted to try to contact Sassy again. At some point we'd need to install a cat door so he could come and go.

Downstairs, I found Drake in the back room fixing a basket full of cheeses, crackers, and wine. He looked up. "What brings you down here?"

"In an effort to be thorough, do you think you could ask Trevor if any of the workers at Merriman Developers were unhappy with his father?"

"Enough to kill the boss, you mean?"

"Yes."

"I'll give him a call."

While Drake did that, I went into the main room. When—and not if—we solved this case, I wanted to have a bottle of wine to celebrate. I found a really nice Cabernet and carried it back to the room.

Drake had finished his call. "Trevor said he is the one who mostly deals with the staff, and they were well paid and happy."

I wasn't really buying it, but Trevor would know. I waved the bottle. "I want to buy this, along with some crackers and Brie."

Drake's brows rose. "Are we celebrating something?"

I wasn't sure what that look was about. "Not yet, but when we figure out who killed Mr. Merriman, Mrs. Merriman will pay us, and your brother and I will be official sleuths. That is, assuming she's not the killer."

He smiled. "I'll make up a nice basket."

"Thank you. Next time I come down, I'll give you my credit card."

"You don't have to do that," he said.

Drake had always been super generous. It was time I pulled my own weight. "I want to."

I trotted back upstairs. To my surprise, Jaxson was there. "Well?" I asked.

"I'm not sure. I was getting mixed signals from her. Since I'm starving, how about we hit up Dolly's diner, and I can tell you everything there?"

I chuckled. "Don't tell me you want to see what Dolly knows about Ms. Samantha Darling?"

"No, but her insight might be useful. Come on."

I turned to Iggy. "Do you want to come?"

He lifted his chest. "Am I the hottest detective in all of Florida?"

I guess that was a yes. "Jump in, then." I held my purse open, and he waddled over.

While I always enjoyed a good meal at my aunt's competition, being with Jaxson would also be nice.

# CHAPTER 9

When Jaxson and I entered the Spellbound Diner, it was rather empty, for which I was glad. It would allow Dolly to spare a few minutes to gossip.

We grabbed a booth, and while we waited for our server, I wanted to hear the dirt on Samantha. "What's the deal on our mystery woman?"

"No surprise, she'd heard her friend had died, and yes, she was rather depressed about it. After all, murder is horrible at any age. Maybe because I spent a few years in prison listening to people claiming they were innocent that I developed a kind of liar radar. I believe she was genuinely sad about Mr. Merriman's death, but she wasn't grief stricken."

"Are you saying they were only friends?"

"Yes, and here's why I'm convinced. On her desk, she had a picture of herself with some good-looking guy who was maybe thirty-five."

"A younger brother maybe?"

Jaxson grinned. "Ah, no. They were looking longingly into each other's eyes."

I had to laugh. Jaxson never seemed to have been the

romantic in high school, but he had changed a lot since then. "Should we rule her out then?"

"Let's move her name to the end of our suspect list. I don't think we should ever take anyone off our radar."

"I agree."

Our server came over. Instead of pouring over the menu, I went with my standard fare of grilled cheese with tomato, fries, and a sweet tea. Jaxson had a lot more control than I did. He picked the grilled fish special and a coffee.

"If Dolly is free, we'd love to see her," I said.

The young girl smiled. "I'll tell her."

While I believed we were on top of the current events, Steve and Nash hadn't been sharing much of anything with us. I was hoping that not only had Pearl called her good friend, Dolly, with the scoop, but other clients as well had shared things with the gossipy diner owner.

When Dolly came out of the back, she was wiping her hands on a towel. "Howdy. I haven't seen you two in a while."

"We've been a bit busy of late."

"I've heard. You have two murders on your hands."

"Yes. We even have our first client," I announced with pride.

"Divinity Merriman. What a shame she's still in jail. I hope they drop the charges soon."

"Me, too," I said. Dolly certainly seemed to be in the loop. Good.

Iggy poked his head out of my purse and glared at me. "Any chance I could have a few lettuce leaves for my buddy here? I forgot to ask the server."

"Absolutely. Be right back."

I looked back at Jaxson. "I'm happy to hear that Dolly doesn't seem to think our client is guilty."

"If not her, then who?" Jax wiggled his brows.

Dolly returned with a plate of greens for Iggy. I placed it

on the seat next to me, and he went to town. "He says thank you."

He hadn't said a thing, but in his defense, he knew she couldn't hear him.

"Tell him he is welcome."

"Dolly, do you have any insight into Mr. Merriman's death?" I asked.

She motioned for Jaxson to move over, and then she slipped in next to him. "The girls and I might have been chatting about it—but not Pearl. Steve has her on lip-lock status."

I worked hard not to laugh. I doubt Pearl could keep her mouth shut if she tried. "Any suspects?"

"My money is on DeWitt Merriman. Why, I remember that boy in high school. He was trouble with a capital T."

"Jaxson was trouble in high school, too, but look at him now—a model citizen."

I swear he blushed.

"That is true. Maude, on the other hand, is convinced it's Olivia."

Her again? "Why is that?"

"Because she's dating some older man, and her father is furious."

Olivia was about thirty. "Do parents really have a say in who their child dates once they turn twenty-one—or in this case, thirty?" I sucked in a breath. "Or is he married?"

"We don't know who he is, but we don't think he's married."

How could anyone carry on a secretive affair these days—especially in Witch's Cove? When we returned to the office, maybe Jaxson could do a little social media search to see if she had shared any photos of the two of them. "That's good to know."

Other than Olivia's possible additional motive, Dolly

didn't seem to know much. Just as she was about to go, her cell rang, the sound a rather cheerful tune.

Her eyes sparkled. "It's Pearl. Let me take this." She swiped the answer button. "What's up?" A few seconds later, her jaw dropped open. "He confessed to killing Loughlin Merriman? Did he say why?" She listened for a good minute. "That makes no sense." She nodded. "Oh, okay. Talk later."

Dolly pressed the off button and placed her phone on the table. "You will not believe who turned himself in."

There weren't many men on our list. "DeWitt?"

"No. Darren Hightower."

Dolly had to have misunderstood. "Why on earth would Darren Hightower kill Mr. Merriman? Are you sure Pearl didn't get mixed up, and Darren confessed to killing his own father?"

"I know what Pearl said."

"What was his motive? He'd need a darn good one."

"Pearl had to whisper, but I think she said he was tired of Mr. Merriman harassing his father to sell the theater."

"That doesn't make much sense. Darren wanted his dad to sell—as did his sister-in-law, for that matter. If someone was a bully, I'd just tell him to stop. I wouldn't kill him. Besides, Darren Hightower is pretty fit. Don't men settle fights with their fists? I don't see him bashing an older guy over the head with a piece of glass."

She shrugged. "I'd say it's thin, but if he didn't kill Merriman, why confess? I don't think anyone was looking at him for it. Were you?"

I looked over at Jaxson. "No."

Someone from behind the counter called Dolly. "Darn. I gotta go."

"Thanks for the update," I said.

"Stop by anytime."

Once she was out of earshot, I wanted to hear Jaxson's opinion. "I didn't see that coming, did you?"

"Not in a million years. Darren wasn't on our who-killed-Merriman board."

"I know, right?"

Our server returned with our drinks and meal. She must have been waiting until the boss lady left our table. "Thanks," I said.

"Steve has to release Mrs. Merriman now," Jaxson said.

"Agreed. I say after we eat, we head on over and make sure he does."

Jaxson smiled, his perfect teeth presenting a very handsome view. Not to mention... I had to stop. We were co-workers, and I had to keep it that way.

As if we both became lost in our own thoughts, we scarfed down our food without commenting on the bizarre situation further. Jaxson tossed his credit card on the table and motioned for the server to come over. I might have said this was a business lunch, but our company had paid for the last few meals, and I had the sense he wanted to do this.

I nodded to the card. "Thank you."

"My pleasure."

Once we settled up, we headed across the street to the sheriff's office, hoping to spring our client. When we stepped inside, Pearl was handing Divinity what I could only guess were her possessions. She was still dressed in the orange two-piece suit, but the clothes she'd arrived in were bloody according to Steve.

Mrs. Merriman looked up, and when she spotted us, hope sprang to her eyes. Behind her in the glass conference room sat Darren Hightower, his head lowered. Poor man. I always liked Darren. Across from him was the sheriff.

I leaned over to Jaxson. "What I wouldn't give to be a fly on that wall."

"No kidding."

Something sharp pressed against my arm and then across my leg. I looked down but saw nothing. I swore it felt like Iggy.

"Iggy, is that you?" I whispered. He must have cloaked himself.

"Shh. Don't give me away. I'll be home when I learn something."

Our office was basically across the street, so I didn't mind if he wanted to look around. I grabbed Jaxson's arm and twisted to face him, not wanting anyone to read my lips. "I think Iggy is planning to sneak into the conference room. He's cloaked himself."

"That's great, but how will he get in?" Jaxson snapped his fingers. "Give me a sec."

He rushed past Pearl and Mrs. Merriman.

"You can't go back there," Pearl called.

"I'll be just a moment."

I couldn't hear anything, but the door to the conference room opened, and I had to assume Iggy would let Jaxson know when he was safely inside. I also didn't know what excuse Jaxson was giving Steve, but Jax smiled and then backed out of the room.

From the cheer in his eyes, he'd done a bit of magic on his own, while enabling our little pink spy to go inside. I probably should have stopped Iggy since we would never hear the end of his big adventure, but I wanted to know the real reason Darren killed Mr. Merriman.

Iggy wouldn't be able to keep cloaked for long, which meant he probably would hide under the table and then uncloak himself. Being very clingy, he could hold onto a table leg for hours and not tire.

With her purse in hand, Mrs. Merriman approached us. "Thank goodness you're here. Can you believe that Darren confessed to killing my husband? Loughlin told me that Darren was the most excited to sell. It makes no sense."

Thank you! "I, too, didn't understand. I'm sure the sheriff will figure it out."

"Do you think one of you could give me a lift home? I'd call one of my children, but..."

I finished her sentence, because it would be difficult for her to say what we were all thinking. "You think Darren might not be guilty but that one of your children could be, right?"

She clasped my arm. "Yes."

"I'll run across the street and get the car," Jaxson said.

I think he was trying to stall to give Iggy more time to listen. Not that it mattered since my iguana couldn't leave until Steve opened the door to escort Darren to the cells. "Thanks, Jax."

No sooner had he rushed out when Olivia Merriman ran in. "Mom? I heard that Darren admitted to killing Dad. Is that true?"

"Apparently."

Olivia was wringing her hands in despair when she should have been hugging her mother. Something wasn't right.

"Why are you here?" I asked. Okay, that wasn't charitable, but too many people had pointed a finger at her. Even her own mother said she didn't totally trust any of her children.

Olivia stood up taller. "Darren called me. I need to speak with him."

Then why ask her mother if Darren had confessed? Not only that, he was given only one phone call. Why contact the daughter of the man he supposedly murdered and not a lawyer? That made no sense. Unless... I glanced over at the man in the glass booth. He was maybe fifty, and he was single. Was he the older man that Olivia might be seeing?

That could explain a few things, especially Darren's motive for killing Olivia's father. But I didn't need to be judging anyone so soon.

Jaxson returned. "Ready?"

"Mom, if you can wait a bit, I can drive you home?"

"That's okay, dear. These nice people have volunteered."

"Okay."

Hopefully, my snoopy, little detective had a good memory and wouldn't need too much bribing to share what he learned.

## CHAPTER 10

"Do you think Iggy got locked into that room?" I asked. It had been an hour since we drove Mrs. Merriman home, and Iggy should have been back by now.

"I'm sure if they left before Iggy could get out, he'd make his presence known," Jaxson said.

"That's true, but can you imagine the stink that would cause? Steve would accuse me of asking my familiar to spy, and he'd be partially right. He'd never believe I didn't send Iggy in."

"Do you want to go look for him?" Jaxson asked.

"Not yet. I wouldn't know what to tell Pearl about why we were there."

He stood. "I'll prop open the office door so he can get in."

Why hadn't I thought of that? As soon as the door opened, Iggy ran in.

"Didn't you hear me scratching?" He bobbed his head. Someone was not a happy camper.

Now I felt terrible. "I'm so sorry. Do you want some water?"

"Yes, please."

*Please?* He rarely used that word.

"I'll get him some," Jaxson offered.

I sat on the sofa, and Iggy jumped on the coffee table, clearly looking forward to taking center stage. "Do tell," I said.

Jaxson returned and placed a bowl of water in front of him. Iggy lapped up some. "Darren Hightower said he was tired of Mr. Merriman bugging his dad."

That wasn't anything new. "Yet the sheriff was aware that Darren wanted his father to sell. Did he ask him about that?"

"Nope. The sheriff barely said anything."

That was probably smart. Steve was a lot better trained at interviewing someone than I was. "Go on."

"Darren explained how he went to Mr. Merriman's office to demand that he stop harassing his dad. Merriman said no. Then came the good part. You're going to love this."

"Iggy." He could go on and on.

"Darren said he only used that as an excuse to kind of break the ice."

"What do you mean?" Jaxson said.

"Apparently, Darren said he and Olivia were going to get married, with or without Mr. Merriman's permission."

I sucked in a breath. "It's true then. Darren Hightower is Olivia's older man friend. I'm assuming Mr. Merriman said over his dead body?"

"More or less."

"And Darren obliged?" Jaxson asked.

"I guess. It was a lengthy discussion that became more and more heated," Iggy said. "Then there was some stuff about motive, and the sheriff asked exactly how the altercation went down. I think Mr. Merriman pushed Darren, and fearing for his life, he picked up the award and hit Mr. Merriman with it, but not really hard. Just enough to show he meant business."

"Yet it was enough to kill him. Darren must not have known his own strength," I said. "Did Mr. Hightower mention that he cleaned off his prints afterward?"

Iggy swung his tail back and forth. "I don't remember, or else it never came up."

"Did Olivia ever go into the room?" Jaxson asked.

"No. The sheriff escorted Darren down some hallway after that. I could hear the lady begging to talk to him, but that didn't happen."

"Wow." I wasn't sure what else to say. I looked over at Jaxson. "I feel sorry for Olivia."

"Because her dad is dead, and her future husband is in jail for killing him?"

"Yes."

He nodded. "I guess that's that then. We're done."

"Yup." It was kind of a letdown, in part because we didn't contribute to the solving of the crime.

The office phone rang, and Jaxson answered. "Pink Iguana Sleuths. How many I help you?" One brow rose. "Of course, Mrs. Merriman. We'll be here." He disconnected. "Our client said she is stopping over to pay us."

"Great. Our first paycheck."

"Since our search for that killer is done, we should celebrate," he said.

"I'd like that, but Darren Hightower turned himself in—without any help from us."

"True. Okay, how's this? After we figure out who killed Darren's dad, we'll celebrate?"

I smiled. "I love that idea. If you don't mind, how about asking Penny and Hunter to go with us? She asked me before if the four of us could go out."

"I'm game."

I hadn't thought he'd be so amenable. "Great." I looked over at Iggy and then back at Jaxson. "What do you think about installing a cat door? I want Iggy to be able to come and go."

"Great idea. I'll stop by the hardware store on my way home."

Was there anything he couldn't do? Before I had the chance to ponder that topic anymore, someone knocked and then pushed open the door. It was Mrs. Merriman who must have called from the parking lot. She'd cleaned up and looked a thousand times better.

I expected a big smile on her face, but instead she rushed up to us.

"Mrs. Merriman, what's wrong?"

"Olivia has just confessed to killing Loughlin."

"What?"

Jaxson moved next to me. "Do you think she killed her own father?"

Because she looked a bit unsteady on her feet, I helped her to the sofa. Jaxson disappeared into the back and returned with a cold bottle of water.

"Thank you. To answer your question, no, I don't think she killed Loughlin. She told me that Darren probably only confessed because he wanted to spare her going to jail."

"He thought she killed her own dad? Some boyfriend he is. Or...did she tell him she did?" I asked. To be fair, it was nice of him to take the fall for something he didn't do, but only if he thought Olivia was guilty.

"I don't know, but I'll pay you double to find out. Our sheriff just tossed them both in jail. I guess he figures one of them will crack."

It was too late to let Iggy spy in the room. Most likely, she'd tell the same tale Darren did, though I don't see her hefting a glass award and then smashing her father over the head with it. Not to be sexist, but women tended more toward using a gun.

"Sure," Jaxson said. "We'll continue to investigate."

I wanted the money, too, but at this point, I didn't understand where we would look or how we could help her. What we needed was a timeline of when he was killed, but I doubted Steve would be willing to share.

From her purse she handed us a check. "This is the first half of your retainer."

As much as I wanted to look at it right now, it would be rude. "Thank you."

Mrs. Merriman stood, and Jaxson escorted her out. Given how long he was out there, he must have waited to be sure she made it down the stairs okay before returning. The poor woman seemed quite distraught.

Jaxson shut the door. "You do realize that we have to be open to the idea that either Darren or Olivia is guilty?"

"I know, but we owe it to Mrs. Merriman to look elsewhere." I wagged a finger. "I'm going to visit my mom."

"Why?"

"I'd like to take a look at the body. Something seems off to me."

"How so?"

"Someone must have let it leak how Mr. Merriman was killed, and both Darren and Olivia are using that information to confess. Otherwise, how would Olivia know how the murder went down—assuming she's innocent?"

"Maybe she talked to Darren at the station," he said.

"Iggy said she didn't, though Darren called her."

"From experience, I can say your one phone call isn't allowed to last a long time. I doubt Darren could tell her every detail of the murder."

"Assuming he was guilty. Regardless, I still want to check if Mom has received Mr. Merriman's body yet."

"He only died yesterday," Jaxson said.

"I don't think Dr. Sanchez has a lot of people to examine."

He held up a hand. "Go. I'll hold down the fort."

"Iggy, are you good to stay with Jaxson?"

He ran around in circles. "Yes. I don't like where your mom keeps the bodies. That place stinks."

I'm glad he finally admitted it. "Okay then. You know where I will be."

I headed downstairs and went next door to the mortuary. I opened the back door and my mom was there, which startled me. "Mom?"

"I was just about to visit you."

That had never happened before. While I wanted to ask about Mr. Merriman's body, this seemed serious. "What is it?"

"Let's go to my office."

Once more, Toto was not around. "Where's your trusty companion?"

"Toto is at the groomers."

"Oh." That made sense, I guess. "Is she okay?"

"Yes. Sit down."

This didn't sound good. "What's going on?"

"It's your Aunt Tricia."

I grabbed the chair, dragged it over to her desk, and dropped down. "Is she okay?" I always feared she'd overdose one day.

"As a matter of fact, she is. She admitted herself to rehab."

My heart lightened. "That's super. Why the long face?"

"She asked if Rihanna could move here and live with us."

"I hadn't seen that coming, but it shouldn't be too bad. She'll be a high school senior and can drive herself everywhere. What's the problem?"

"We have no room here. Your old room is now your father's office."

While the funeral home part of the building was nice and large, the upstairs was small. "What are you suggesting? And don't say she can move in with me. I only have one bedroom."

"I thought she could bunk in your office. It has a small kitchen and a bathroom."

While there was a backroom, it was full of all of Drake's stuff. "I don't think that will work."

"Why not?"

The last thing I needed was to get into an argument with my mother. Those never ended well. I always walked away feeling guilty. "I'm twenty-six."

"Almost twenty-seven," she reminded me.

"Fine. Almost twenty-seven. Here's the thing. I know nothing about raising a teenager." Rihanna was only seventeen.

My mother reached out and clasped my hand. "Think about it, okay? She'll be here tomorrow."

What? "Do you think she should be around Jaxson?" That was lame, but I had to think of something.

"What's wrong with him?"

Nothing. I refused to believe I might be jealous. "He's an ex-con," I blurted.

"He was innocent. You just don't want to be responsible for her."

That was true, too. "You're right. I don't, but we'll figure something out. On a different note, did Dr. Sanchez finish the autopsy on Loughlin Merriman?" That abrupt change of subject might have sounded callous, but I needed time to think.

"She did. He's downstairs."

"Good. I want to take a look at him."

"Why? His cause of death is clear. He died from blunt force trauma to the head."

At some point, I'd like to see this massive award. Did it weigh ten pounds or something? "I know."

"Go ahead. He's in drawer three."

I really disliked how clinical that sounded. Wanting to get away from my mom's accusing eyes, I rushed to the embalming room. I called it our morgue because it sounded nicer for some reason. By now, I should be used to seeing dead bodies, but some of the dead affected me more than others.

I pulled open drawer three. From the top, Mr. Merriman looked quite good, if I ignored the Y-shaped incision in his chest. I slid the table under the drawer and transferred him for a better look. It was probably the light, but a slight bruising appeared near his temple. I wonder why Steve forgot to mention that.

With difficulty, I rolled him onto his side to get a look at the back of his head. Wow. The gash was huge. No wonder he died. While I was no expert, I'd have to say Olivia didn't have the upper body strength to strike her dad that hard. Darren on the other hand, did. With that kind of force, I would've thought the award would have cracked under that much stress, and Mrs. Merriman never mentioned any glass had broken.

I rolled the body back and then returned Mr. Merriman to the cooler.

Normally, I would have gone back to my mom's office to ask her to try to contact either Mr. Merriman or Mr. Hightower from beyond once more, but she wasn't happy with me right now. I needed a friendly face.

As much as I knew I should return to the office and tell Jaxson about this new development with my cousin, as well as the massive gash on Mr. Merriman's head, I decided to return to my apartment, wash up, and call Penny, as it would be her day off.

I really needed an unbiased, friendly chat where no demands would be heaped upon me.

## CHAPTER 11

Penny said once she dropped Tommy off at her mother's, she'd meet me at Maude's tea shop.

"See you there," I said.

I was excited to have a girl chat. All this death was getting to me. As was the idea of taking on my cousin, a teenager who was nothing like me when I was her age. Thinking of Rihanna, I needed to let Jax know that I would be stopping by later than I'd planned to pick up Iggy, so I called him.

"Don't worry about it," he said. "After I stop at the hardware store for the cat door, how about I take him back to my place? We'll have a boy's night."

I chuckled at the image of them hanging out. "You are the best."

"I try."

No doubt about it. Jaxson Harrison was getting to me, and I had to stop this stupid attraction from going any further. I couldn't afford to lose him as my business partner. Sure, things might not end in catastrophe, but why chance it? I'd never been able to keep a boyfriend for long in the past. Besides, who was to say Jaxson wanted to date me anyway?

After I changed my clothes, I headed over to the Moon Bay Tea Shop and was happy to see that Maude had a fair amount of customers. I grabbed my usual table near the window and waited for Penny.

Before my friend arrived, the owner rushed over. "Glinda, can you believe what's been happening in this town?"

I didn't want to pretend ignorance on this one. "I know, right? Two murders and two confessions in the span of like two days."

"What's even crazier is that Steve released both Darren and Olivia a few minutes ago."

My heart raced. "What? Why?"

She held up her hands. "He said they didn't do it."

Really? "Does that mean he knows who did?" And here I thought things couldn't get any zanier.

She stood up straighter and planted a hand on her hip. "If he does, he's not saying."

If he wasn't talking, then Pearl couldn't learn anything, which meant Maude was out of the loop, too.

Before I could ask any more questions, Penny rushed in, smiled, and waved. From her cheery attitude, she probably hadn't heard about all this mess.

My friend slipped in across from me. "Hey, Maude."

"Penny. Nice to see you again."

Before Maude left or brought up anything about the murders, I wanted to order. I really needed that sugar hit. "I'd like an apple cinnamon green iced tea and two chocolate chip cookies, please."

Penny ordered a black tea and an apple scone. As soon as Maude left to place our order, Penny turned to me. "What's new?"

I laughed. "What's not new?"

For the next few minutes, I regaled her with all the comings and goings of the two murders, what I learned about the body, and the fact my cousin might be moving in with me.

"Wow. You've had a tough day."

"Tell me about it."

One of their servers delivered our order, and boy did that first cookie taste divine. It was just what my brain needed. The problem was as soon as I ate the second one, I would be tempted to order a half dozen more. Decisions, decisions. With Iggy on his sleepover, I might need some comfort food for later. A to-go box it was.

Penny waved her glass at me. "If neither Darren nor Olivia killed Mr. Merriman, who did?"

"I have no idea," I said. "I never would have picked Darren in the first place, but my money had been on Olivia." That was probably because so many people had pointed the finger at her.

"What about the Hightower murder? Any leads on that?"

I loved that Penny was so interested in what I did. "I'm at a loss there too, but I was hoping you could ask Hunter to do us a favor."

"What's that?"

"It's possible that nuts from the Barbados Nut tree poisoned Mr. Hightower. I'd like to know if that tree grows in the forest or someplace nearby."

"What does it look like?"

I could never describe it, so I pulled it up on my phone. "Here it is. The leaves kind of look like ivy." I read the description, but it sounded like all trees to me.

"Hunter is really knowledgeable. He might know."

"Thanks. If they are poisonous, I doubt the nuts would be sold in stores. Perhaps the person who gave them to Mr. Hightower claimed they were a delicacy or thought they were." I had read one or two things about them having medicinal properties, but maybe the nuts had to be processed for any benefits to be realized.

Penny took a bite out of her apple scone. "If we assume that is what killed him, even if you locate the tree, how does that help you find out who gave him the nuts?"

"It doesn't really. Not unless someone saw this person pick the nuts off the tree, or if he bought the nuts and had them shipped in. That means I need to find an eye witness."

"What about asking your mother to contact Mr. Hightower. Maybe he can tell her who gave him the nuts," Penny said.

I shook my head. "She said she can't make the dead talk. They have to want to be contacted. Even then, she often gets a lot of misinformation."

Penny chuckled. "Even if Mr. Hightower told your mom that Mr. X killed him, it wouldn't exactly stand up in a court of law, now would it?"

That was the problem with all paranormal leads. "No."

While I polished off my drink, Penny finished her scone.

"Have you figured out what you're going to do with your cousin when she arrives tomorrow?" Penny asked.

"No."

I stuffed my last whole cookie in my mouth, hoping the intense burst of sugar would bring me some clarity. It did not. Jaxson was always my go-to guy, but I didn't want to burden him with my family issues. I was hoping that with a good night's sleep, I might have some clearer thoughts tomorrow.

After Penny and I chatted about Rihanna's upcoming visit, we spent some time talking about how wonderful Hunter was, even though he worked too hard. When she mentioned that Tommy, her seven-year old, would be starting second grade in a few weeks, I couldn't believe it. I swear his fourth birthday party was just yesterday.

After we finished, we hugged goodbye, and I went back to my empty apartment. It was strange and sad knowing that Iggy would not be crawling through that cat door at any minute. As ornery as he could be sometimes, I loved him. The only consolation was that Iggy would probably enjoy total freedom with Jaxson. I wouldn't be surprised if they watched some sports game on the tube tonight.

I inhaled, trying to focus on the positive. Having the place to myself would give me some time to think about my options with my cousin. How did I want to handle Rihanna? Once she settled in though, I'd have to refocus my efforts on trying to find the real killers.

To help clear my thoughts, I decided to go with an easy microwaveable dinner and then indulge in a nice hot bath, before settling down with a good book—and the rest of the chocolate chip cookies.

---

WHEN I WALKED into the office the next morning, Iggy seemed agitated. "What's wrong? Did you miss me that much?" I could only hope.

He spun to face me. "Sure, but that's not the problem. It's Sassy."

"What about her?"

"She won't leave me alone."

"What are you talking about?" I knew very little about ghosts, and even less about animal ghosts, but I doubted she had the ability to stay around for very long. That would take a lot of energy on her part.

"When Jaxson and I arrived this morning, she was here."

"In the office?" I asked.

"Yes, that's what *here* means."

"You don't have to snap at me." I couldn't see or hear her, which frustrated me, especially since I was a witch. "Where is Sassy now?" I asked.

"On the sofa."

"Which end?" I certainly didn't want to sit on her.

"Left." He pointed to what he called the left end.

As long as she was here, I might as well see what she knew. "Can you ask her if Mr. Hightower was allergic to nuts?"

"She can hear you, but only I can understand her answer." Iggy faced the sofa. "No, he loved nuts. All kinds."

Which was why he was willing to taste some. "Sassy, who visited Mr. Hightower in the last few months?" I imagine that when Sassy was alive, she was rather social.

Iggy hopped up on the coffee table and faced one end of the sofa. Now I understood what other people went through when I spoke to Iggy. He listened for a bit and then faced me. "Mostly Amanda and sometimes Darren."

"What about Mr. Merriman?" The developer was murdered after Mr. Hightower. He could have killed Sassy's owner, though she would have been in her ghost form by then.

Iggy waited, but this time his tail was thumping, a sure sign he was losing patience. He faced me. "Yes."

"When was the last time she saw him?"

"She doesn't remember," he said, clearly not liking being a go-between.

"Anyone else visit while she was among the living?" I asked. It somehow seemed easier to ask Iggy.

"Mr. Plimpton came once or twice. But that was a while ago. He was trying to get her owner to sell the theater since Mr. Plimpton really wanted to get out of the ice cream business," Iggy said, translating for Sassy.

That was consistent with what I'd already learned. "No one else? A neighbor perhaps?" I was desperate for a lead.

"Mrs. Elderberry," Iggy said to me then turned back to his ghost. "Who's she?" he asked Sassy. "Oh. She's a neighbor, but she's older than Mr. Hightower."

She could have given him the nuts thinking they were safe. The issue with that was if she'd visited him that fateful day, Mr. Hightower would have used his delicate china tea set instead of manly mugs.

"Tell her thank you."

Jaxson came up the back staircase. "Hey, Glinda."

I turned to Jaxson. "I'm glad you're here. I need to discuss something with you. And Iggy."

"What's up?" Jaxson asked.

I explained about my aunt being the black sheep of the family and why. "She entered rehab, but her seventeen-year old daughter needs a place to live for a few months."

His eyebrows rose. "And she wants to move here?"

"We're her only relatives."

"Okay, what's the problem?" Jaxson asked.

"There's no room at the funeral home, and I only have a one bedroom. Where am we going to put her?"

"She can sleep on the couch in our living room," Iggy said.

It would sound uncharitable if I said I liked my space. "I don't think she'd like that. Kids need their privacy."

"I have an idea," Jaxson said. "What if you and your cousin stay at my place, which is a two-bedroom, and I move into your apartment?"

Iggy did two circles. "I'll stay with Jaxson."

My mouth opened. "You are a little traitor. One night with Jaxson and you're ready to jump ship?"

He lifted his leg, as if to say, whatever.

"Thank you for the generous offer, Jaxson. I'll think about

it." I was rather spoiled living so close to the restaurant, my parents, and our office.

"If not my place, what about here?" he asked. "She'd be well supervised, at least during the day when she's not at school. If she needs anything, she can always ask Drake or Trace for help. Besides, you are only two buildings away."

I looked around. He had a good point. "The sofa isn't a pull-out, though I guess we could buy one."

"Kids usually don't mind crashing anywhere, but long term, I was thinking about that back room."

While this second floor had been built as an apartment, the back bedroom was stuffed with junk from floor to ceiling. "And you are planning to throw out Drake's prized possessions?"

He smiled. "No, my brother would have my head. I was thinking we could rent a storage unit. I'm sure I could find a couple of guys to move the stuff out."

"Wow. That would be fantastic, but Rihanna is coming tomorrow."

"Then I better have a heart-to-heart with my little brother."

"I'll join you."

I turned to Iggy. "You better stay here and take care of Sassy."

He bobbed his head at me, clearly unhappy. "See if I ask her any more questions for you."

I'd had enough. "Iggy, behave." I turned back to Jaxson. "Let's go."

We found Drake downstairs and explained the situation.

"Sure. It will do me good to look through everything and see what's there. I can probably toss half of it. Since Trace is working today, I'll help."

That was win-win. "We'll pay for the storage unit, of course," I said.

"That works."

"While you two he-men take care of that, I'd like to stop over at the sheriff's office."

"Glinda?" Jaxson sounded leery.

"I looked at Mr. Merriman's body and had some questions. I wanted to share my thoughts with him."

"Okay."

I appreciated that Jaxson was always looking out for me, but I didn't need his permission to do my job.

Trusting the two brothers had everything under control, I headed across the street. When I entered the sheriff's department, Pearl looked up from her receptionist desk and smiled. "Hey there. Did you hear?" she whispered.

"That your grandson released our two confessors?"

"Yes."

"I did. It's what I want to talk to Steve about. Is he in?"

"Sure. Go on back."

Sadly, the sheriff's department almost felt like home. I knocked on Steve's door and entered.

He put down his pen and looked up. "Glinda. Do you have another suspect for me to check out?"

He could have been referring to either murder case. "Not exactly." I pulled up a chair and sat down. "I was about to prepare Mr. Merriman's body when I noticed something interesting."

Yes, I know, I wasn't going to fix him up for a viewing, but I didn't want Steve to think less of me for prying.

"And?"

"Two things struck me as odd. One was the bruise on Mr. Merriman's temple, and the other was the huge gash on the back of the man's head. I've not seen this glass award, nor am I a medical examiner, but I don't think the gash came from someone just hitting him over the head with it."

Steve leaned back in his chair. "You're right."

## CHAPTER 12

"I'm right?" I hadn't expected Steve to admit anything about the crime.

He crossed his arms. "Since you have figured out the major reason why I had to let Darren Hightower and Olivia Merriman go, I'll tell you that the gash at the back of his head came from hitting the corner of his desk, and not from any glass award as I first thought. I'll blame myself for not seeing the dried blood on the wooden desk in the first place. I'm not sure what really happened in that room, but so far no one has come up with a scenario that fits the crime scene."

"Do you have an explanation for why there are no additional fingerprints on the award?"

"The award might not have anything to do with the murder. Who's to say it wasn't cleaned a day or two beforehand and then knocked over in the altercation?"

That made sense. "What about the bruise to Mr. Merriman's temple? I'm assuming that was in the autopsy report?"

"It was. From the amount of bruising, Dr. Sanchez thinks he was hit maybe thirty minutes before he died."

I wasn't sure what that meant. "Whoever hit him might not have killed him then?"

"I can't say."

He couldn't say or he wouldn't say. "Because?"

Steve actually smiled. "Because I don't know. Mr. Merriman might have been in a small altercation with someone who hit him. That person left, and a second person came in and shoved Mr. Merriman, who fell and hit his head."

"Resulting in his death."

"Yes," Steve said.

"Did the medical examiner give you a time of death?"

He huffed—a sure sign he was rather exasperated with me. "Six p.m., give or take a half hour."

"When did Olivia say she was in his office—assuming she ever spoke with her dad?"

"She couldn't remember."

"That was convenient." All I had to do was ask Mrs. Merriman to drag the truth out of her daughter. Since Steve didn't seem to want to tell me more, it was time to leave. "If I can help in any way, let me know."

"If I'm convinced a ghost killed Mr. Merriman, or a witch put a deadly spell on him, you'll be the first to know."

That was rather snarky of him, but he was probably as frustrated as I was. I pushed my chair back and left.

When I entered the Pink Iguana Sleuth's office from the inside stairwell, it was rather chaotic. About six guys were hauling stuff out through the front door and down the outside staircase.

"Jaxson," I called.

He popped his head out of the back. "You called, boss?"

"I did. You don't need to call me boss. We are partners." I waved a hand around the room. "You moved fast."

"You said Rihanna is arriving tomorrow."

"I did, so thank you."

Drake came out of the back with Trevor, both carrying a large box. When they stepped around the sofa, Trevor winced.

"Gotta rest for a second," he said.

They set the box down, and Trevor rubbed his ribcage. It was clear he was in pain. I stepped over to him. "What's wrong?"

"Got sucker punched in the ribs. I think I cracked something."

"Then you should be resting."

He chuckled. "I'll survive." He turned back to Drake. "Let's go."

I watched for a bit, thrilled that Jaxson and Drake were so agreeable to helping me clear out the space. Having a room for Rihanna was actually going to happen.

Wanting to say thank you to everyone who helped, I headed to the Tiki Hut where I bought several desserts along with some cold beer. I took everything upstairs, set out the cookies, and placed the beer in the fridge.

Wanting to help with the cleaning out process, I carried out as many boxes as I could into the living room, all the while Iggy just watched. "How's Sassy doing?" I asked him.

"She's still here. She said she won't leave my side until we find out who killed Mr. Hightower. Maybe having Detective on my nameplate wasn't such a good idea after all. The stress is substantial."

I laughed. "You are a hoot."

"I'm not an owl."

"No, you are not." I'm glad I'd never seen an owl on our beach or Iggy might become dinner one day.

When everyone returned, I offered them the snacks, for which they were appreciative.

"I think I'll hire someone to move the bedroom furniture

from my place to here," Jaxson said. "I've used up my good will for a while. Free labor is tough to find."

"I get it." I moved closer to him. "Something has been bothering me."

"What? You're afraid to tell me I need a shower?"

I laughed and then punched him in the arm. For sure, it hurt me more than him. "No. It was something Steve said about Mr. Merriman's death."

"What is it?"

"How about you ask Drake and Trevor to stay behind after everyone else leaves?"

"You don't think Trevor killed his father, do you?" Jaxson kept his voice low.

"No, but...it's too hard to explain."

"Okay."

As the men were about to leave, I thanked them once more.

"Hey, Trevor?" Jaxson asked. "Can you and Drake stay for a minute?"

"Sure. You need something else moved?"

Trevor was a good guy. "No. I want to talk to you," I said.

Trevor and Drake took a seat. Now came the hard part. "I thought you should know what I found out about your father's death." He sat up straighter and then winced. "Who punched you, Trevor?"

He shook his head. "It was a stupid argument."

"With?"

"My father."

I tried not to let my disappointment show. "What happened?" His lips pressed together. "If you want to learn what happened to your dad, please tell me."

He leaned back against the sofa and held up his hands. "Okay. Fine. To be honest, I was fed up with my father always trying to control my life."

That sounded like motive for murder to me. "Because he wanted you to go into the business instead of pursuing your dream?"

"Yes! Exactly. The thing is, Olivia is far more qualified than I am to run the business, which meant I wouldn't have been leaving him in the lurch. And DeWitt, while a screw up sometimes, is really good at marketing."

"Did you talk to your dad the day he died or something?" I tried to sound totally non-judgmental, but I'm not sure if I succeeded.

"I did."

I didn't ask him what time this discussion took place. I'd bring it up later.

"What caused him to punch you?" Jaxson asked.

"He wasn't exactly thrilled when I told him I was leaving Witch's Cove."

"Ouch," I said. "I can see where that would upset him. He probably thought it was a slap in the face."

"It's what kids are supposed to do. Grow up and make their own lives. I had to let him know how I felt, and that I couldn't live *his* dream anymore."

"I get that. Trust me, I do," I said. "If my parents had their way, I'd have a safe and respectable job. It wouldn't be waitressing or be an amateur sleuth."

"I hear you," he said.

I leaned forward. "After he punched you in the ribs, what did you do?" Steve's words came back to me.

"I just reacted. I punched him back. Once, and then he screamed at me to get out."

"That's it?" I asked.

"Yeah. Dad was fine when I left. I swear."

"What time was this?" Sorry, I had to ask.

"I'd say about quarter past five. I remember, because I

work in the office down the hall, and I waited until Doris left at five before talking to him. She's our receptionist."

I wanted to believe him, but his dad's time of death lined up too well. "Why didn't you tell the sheriff about your altercation?"

"Why would I have? It was nothing. My dad sucker punched me—and trust me, it wasn't the first time."

"Has he ever cracked one of your ribs before?" I asked.

"No. At the last second, I saw the swing coming and twisted to get out of the way. Instead of him hitting my stomach, his fist caught my ribcage. It was my fault."

"I've been in more fights than I care to admit," Jaxson said. "Sometimes, you just react. It's something you don't even think twice about."

"Totally."

"When you left, your dad was fine. Is that why you thought Olivia must have killed him?" I asked.

"Someone did. Besides, the night before, she told me she was going to confront Dad about how poorly he'd been treating her. I didn't know about her and Darren at the time."

"Thanks for letting us know. We're still no closer to figuring out how your dad died." I certainly wasn't going to mention that his father somehow hit his head on the corner of the desk.

"Trevor did nothing wrong," Drake said.

"I never claimed he did. I only asked because I was worried about his injury."

Drake dipped his chin, clearly not believing me, but it was true. Mostly.

Trevor waved his beer. "Thanks for the cookies and beer. I need to get going."

"Sure." I stood. "You said you planned to go back to school. I trust that's still the plan?"

"It is. Once this mess with dad is cleared up, and my family heals a bit, I'll reapply."

I held out my hand. "I wish you luck."

After Drake escorted Trevor out, my good friend returned. "What was with the interrogation?" Drake asked.

"I wanted to know why he had a cracked rib."

"Glinda, please."

I didn't want to think I was picking on Trevor. "Fine. Here's the scoop."

I explained my observations of Mr. Merriman's body and what Steve told me about the time of death.

"You think Trevor punched him more than once and killed him?" Drake asked.

"No. I think Trevor told the truth."

"But?"

"Steve thought someone else could have come in for an office chat—obviously after Trevor left, shoved Mr. Merriman hard enough to cause him to hit his head on the desk. He then bled out."

"Does he have a suspect?" Drake asked.

"No. I'm guessing that since neither Olivia nor Darren mentioned Mr. Merriman hitting his head on the desk, they were trying to cover for each other."

"Now what?" Jaxson asked.

"I don't know."

"Are you going to mention Trevor's interaction to Steve?" Drake asked.

"Maybe, but not now. The whole thing could have been completely innocent. I'm sure both of you have gotten into some fisticuffs and didn't think anything about it."

"For sure," Jaxson said.

I kind of doubted Drake had been in any kind of brawl, but who knows.

"Here's my take," I said. "We have no evidence that Trevor

shoved his dad in such a way that caused his father to hit his head on the desk's edge, pass out, and die."

Drake and Jaxson looked at each other. "Agreed," Drake said.

"Are we good then?" Jaxson asked.

"For now."

Jaxson stood. "If that is all, Detective Goodall, I need to make arrangements to have some of my bedroom furniture delivered tomorrow."

Without thinking, I hugged him. "Thank you."

I immediately stepped back. The hug felt too good.

Drake stood. "And I need to check on Trace."

The air was a little uncomfortable in the room. "I'm going next door to check on the details of when Rihanna is expected." I would ask my mom about my cousin and then ask whether she'd been successful contacting either Mr. Merriman or Mr. Hightower from the beyond. Hopefully, both had answered.

## CHAPTER 13

I found my mother in her office staring off into space. Thankfully, Toto was back, but for once, she didn't bark at me. That wasn't good. It meant she was worried about my mother.

"Mom?"

She snapped out of her stupor and looked up at me. "Glinda! I didn't hear you come in."

I rushed over to the spare chair and sat down. "What's wrong? Is it Aunt Tricia?"

"Oh, no. It's Mr. Merriman, I think."

I couldn't imagine what that could be about. "Tell me."

"It's never happened before."

"What's never happened?" I was beginning to worry about her.

"I tried contacting Mr. Hightower."

Excitement shot through me. "That's great. What did he say?"

"He didn't answer."

"Oh. You said something about Mr. Merriman?" My mother had never been this confused before.

"I did. I reached out to Mr. Hightower, but instead Mr. Merriman answered. At least I think it was Mr. Merriman."

That didn't sound good. "What did this mystery man say?"

"He said to tell Trevor that he was sorry. That it was his fault."

"Did he say what he was sorry for?" I asked. Too often the information was garbled, causing my mother to have to interpret it.

"No. He left before I could question him more fully."

I had to think about that. I could decode the first half. Trevor wanted to pursue his own dreams, and his father had prevented him for his own gain. But what was his fault? And did that mean it was Trevor's fault or Mr. Merriman's fault?

"Is this the first time someone other than the intended person you tried to contact answered?"

"Yes."

That would be upsetting. "I'll speak to Trevor about it and see if he can figure it out."

She looked up at me, and a bit of sparkle returned to her eyes. "Thank you."

I wanted to cheer her up. "I have news."

"What is it, sweetie?"

"Drake and Jaxson put all of Drake's extra stuff from the backroom upstairs into storage. Now we have a spare bedroom in the office where Rihanna can stay."

"That's wonderful. You'll be able to keep a watch on her during the day too, but it won't look like you're spying on her."

That was one way of looking at it. "I guess so, but she will be on her own at night."

"Your dad and I are only a few feet away if she needs anything. Or you can ask Iggy to check on her every once in a while. He is a sneaky thing."

I laughed. "He is at that. I bet he would love to have such

an important role, though right now he has his hands full, what with Sassy not leaving his side."

"Sassy, Mr. Hightower's ghost cat?"

"Yup."

My mother's lips firmed. "Maybe she can ask her owner to contact me."

I chuckled. "Somehow, I don't think it works that way, but I'll be happy to ask."

"Thanks." My mom's phone rang.

"Go ahead and take that, but call me when Rihanna arrives."

"I will."

When I left, my head was spinning. I had to let Trevor know what my mom found out. Whether he'd believe me was a different matter. It was hard for some people to accept the word of a witch. I was just hoping if he did, it would give him some closure.

Back at the office, two men were delivering the bedroom furniture from Jaxson's house. He had obviously found someone to head out to his place right away. "You are a miracle worker," I told him.

"If I were a seventeen-year old girl, I'd appreciate a room to myself, instead of being forced to sleep on some short couch. I know you want to make her welcome."

"That is sweet of you. I have some pink sheets I can bring over."

Jaxson laughed. "I'm sure you do."

"Got a minute?"


"Sure, what's up?"

We had to move out of the way as two men in uniform carried in a dresser. I wouldn't be surprised if this room was nicer than the one she had at home. Only then did it occur to me that in the next couple of days, I'd have to enroll her in school. Yikes. That sounded a lot like motherhood, and I wasn't sure I was ready for that.

"Glinda?"

"Oh, yeah. My mom spoke with Mr. Merriman."

He clasped my arm. "Sit down and tell me."

I explained how upset she was that when she tried to contact Mr. Hightower, Mr. Merriman showed up instead. "That's never happened to her before."

"I don't see the issue. Both men are dead."

"I kind of felt the same way, but apparently my mother did not. Anyway, I think Trevor would like to hear what his dad had to say. It was about him."

"I can ask Drake to contact him."

"That would be great."

While Jaxson texted his brother, Iggy hopped up on the coffee table. "So, no news about who killed Mr. Hightower?" he asked.

"It's possible it was all a mistake. If the nuts were responsible for his death, someone might have given them to him without knowing the side effects."

Iggy looked to the side. "Okay, okay." He turned back to me. "Sassy doesn't believe it. The death threat means someone meant to kill him."

"Okay, Mr. Sleuth, with Mr. Merriman dead, who's left besides his son, his daughter-in-law, or a possible creditor?"

"I'm voting for Darren," Iggy said.

"And why is that?" Sometimes Iggy had good ideas. It was also possible that Sassy had been telling him things about her owner that would help.

"You said Darren and Olivia Merriman plan to marry, right?"

"Yes. What about it?"

"If Darren wanted Olivia to succeed, wouldn't it be great if he got his dad to agree to sell the theater?" Iggy asked.

"I guess."

"I would bet that building a condo is a big deal. Look how much work it took for you guys to clear out one room."

"Your point?" I asked.

"Mr. Merriman might have asked Trevor to do most of the work, but Olivia could play a vital role, which would allow her dad to see how good she is."

"Makes sense."

Jaxson put away his phone and leaned in. "I see where Iggy is going with this. Darren could be our man. He had the means, assuming he could locate the fairly poisonous nuts. He had the motive, which was to prove to Mr. Merriman that Olivia should run the company. And he had the opportunity. He visited his father on a regular basis. No one would pay any attention to his comings and goings."

"What Jaxson said," Iggy added.

"It all sounds good, but how do we prove it?"

"That is the rub," Jax said.

"I'm sure the sheriff looked into Darren's whereabouts right before Mr. Hightower's death."

"I'm sure he did," Jaxson said.

I nodded to his phone. "Will Trevor text you if he is coming over?"

"He will."

"What about Amanda as the killer?" I asked. "I heard she was loose with her money and even gambled. She'd need the inheritance as quickly as possible."

"Amanda, Amanda," Iggy chanted.

"Wishing someone guilty won't help," I said. My familiar sure was fickle. First, he believed Darren was guilty, and now he's voting for Amanda. I turned back to Jaxson. "You said that Mr. Hightower had taken out some loans in recent years. Were his payments up-to-date?"

"They were, which probably means it wasn't some creditor who was after him."

Darn. Darren or Amanda? Why was this case so hard? Not that we'd figured out Merriman's case yet either.

Jaxson's phone pinged. "It's Trevor. He's stopping over."

"Good. After he leaves, I need to get the room ready for Rihanna. Then I can start asking around about our two dead men."

"Now that Olivia is free, Mrs. Merriman should be happy," he said. "I imagine we'll get the second part of our fee shortly."

"Yes." For everyone's sake, I was hoping we wouldn't have to point the finger at her younger son.

I didn't mention that Trevor's punch might have caused his dad's death, even if it was in self-defense. I would be happy when this was resolved.

It wasn't long before someone knocked on our office door, and Trevor walked in. "Hey, guys. Glinda, you said you had a message or something from my dad?"

I hoped that Jaxson told him the message came after his father had passed. "Yes. Have a seat. Did you know that my mother can contact those who've passed over?"

"Drake mentioned it."

"She was actually contacting Mr. Hightower when your dad joined the group chat, so to speak."

His brows rose. "Okay."

I could tell Trevor was being polite. He probably wanted to tell me I was crazy, but I think part of him really wanted it to be true. I pulled a piece of paper from my pocket. Not wanting to forget anything Mom said, I had written down his father's words. "Just so you know, the deceased person doesn't always make sense, but this is what my mom heard." I handed him the paper.

He read it. "I wonder what he's sorry for?"

"It could be for holding you back and not letting you pursue your dreams," Jaxson said.

"Could be."

"Maybe for losing control and punching you?" That was all I could offer right then.

"Okay. The first part could refer to a lot of things, but the part about whose fault it was, did he mean me or him?"

Since Trevor seemed quite upset, I went with the kinder explanation. "It could mean your dad was sorry for pushing you so hard to stay and run the business, or maybe he was admitting it was his fault for not taking his medications which ultimately ended with him dying after you had left." Or it could mean it was Trevor's punch that caused him to fall and hit his head a little while later and die.

"I see. Thank you for this."

"Sure."

"I think I'll talk to the sheriff to see what he can make of it," Trevor said.

Really? That was putting a lot of faith into Sheriff Rocker's hands. It also implied Trevor probably hadn't killed his father—or think he was in any way responsible. If he was, he wouldn't tell the law that he'd been in his father's office about thirty minutes before he died. "I hope he can help."

Once Trevor left, I spent the next few hours fixing up Rihanna's bedroom. She'd need towels, sheets, and toiletries like soap and shampoo. I had to say, it was almost fun making up a room from scratch.

When I was done, I was beat. "I'm heading home," I told Jaxson.

"Okay. If I hear anything from Trevor, I'll let you know."

"Thanks." I turned to Iggy. "Ready?"

"Are you kidding? I can't wait to get away from Sassy."

"Why do you think she won't follow us? It's not like she's confined to four walls."

"Ugh."

Iggy hopped into my purse and off we went.

---

The next morning, when we returned to the office, Sassy was still there, probably ready to pester poor Iggy.

Around noon, I received a text from my mother saying that she and Rihanna were coming up to the office. "My cousin will be here soon," I told Iggy. No doubt Sassy heard too.

"I'm excited," Iggy said.

"I'm glad. I know she'll adore you."

"Yeah. Everyone does."

When had my familiar become so egotistical? "Rihanna is part witch. She'll be able to understand you, so no snarky comments, okay?"

"No snarky comments. I get it." He bobbed his head.

I didn't believe it for a moment. "Don't sass me, or I'll lock you in a small room where you and Sassy can spend the rest of your lives." Sure, that was cruel, but sometimes I had to take harsh measures.

"You wouldn't dare."

"Watch me," I said.

Someone knocked and then the door opened. Here goes!

## CHAPTER 14

When my cousin walked in behind my mom, wearing a ragged backpack, the dejection and vacant look in her eyes broke my heart. At that moment, I was determined to make this the best thing ever for her.

"Rihanna, I'm glad you made it."

She looked around. "Me, too," Rihanna said without much enthusiasm.

"Let me show you to your room and where you can freshen up." I turned to my mother. "Do you want to fix us some iced tea? I have a pitcher in the fridge."

The kitchen was bare bones, but it had a microwave, a sink, some counter space, and a half-sized refrigerator.

"Sure."

I led Rihanna to the makeshift bedroom. I had to hand it to myself for making it so cozy.

"It's pink." She looked back at me.

To be fair, I might have gone a little overboard. "We can go shopping for a black bedspread if that would be better."

"Sure."

Rihanna was at least five-feet ten inches and weighed no

more than one hundred and twenty pounds. Even at five-foot three, I weighed more than that. Where my hair was blonde, hers was black, though I had the sense she had some help with that color. The nose stud was rather tastefully done, but I could do without the eyebrow piercing. Being a hip twenty-six-year old, I kept my mouth shut.

"The bathroom is next door. We all share it during office hours."

"You work here?"

I thought the desks would have given it away. "We do."

"We?"

"I have a partner."

At that moment, Iggy pranced in. "Hi, Rihanna."

Her eyes lit up. "Iggy. I haven't seen you in ages." She bent down and lifted him up. "Oh, my. Love the leather collar."

"Thanks." He turned back to me. "Can I have a body piercing too?"

This wasn't good. "Where would you like it?" I asked him.

Of course, I was kidding, but if he could bluff, so could I.

"How about on my tail? If I slapped someone, it would hurt."

That was what I was afraid of. "Maybe when you turn twenty-one."

He crawled up to Rihanna's shoulder, probably to show me his dissatisfaction. Fine.

"Take off your pack, Rihanna, and make yourself at home. I wrote down the Wi-Fi code on that sticky note. If you want to wash up, we'll be in the main room. Come on Iggy. Let's give her some privacy."

She handed me my slightly angry animal. I would let my cousin do whatever she needed to do, while I returned to where my mother was placing the drinks on the coffee table.

"I put a plate out for Iggy," she said.

"Thank you." Though I wasn't sure the traitor deserved it.

I placed him on the table, grabbed my drink, and dropped down onto one of the two chairs. Just then Jaxson came up through the inner staircase. "Did I hear voices?" he said with a smile on his face.

"Yes. Mom and Rihanna are here. My cousin is washing up."

"Hello, Jaxson," my mom said. "Can I get you a tea?"

"I'll grab a soda. Thanks."

Sweet tea wasn't his thing. When Jaxson returned, Rihanna came out in what looked like a different outfit. It was still all black, but I certainly wasn't one to complain. Perhaps color fetishes ran in the family. The moment she saw Jaxson, she stopped in her tracks.

"Whoa. Who are you?"

It was hard to miss the interest in her eyes.

Being the gentleman that he was, Jaxson jumped up and held out is hand. "Jaxson Harrison. I'm your cousin's partner. Business partner, that is."

Did he really have to clarify? From the hunger in her seventeen-year-old eyes, she wanted to eat him up. Truthfully, I couldn't blame her.

Jaxson moved to the chair next to me and motioned Rihanna take the sofa. "What are your hobbies, Rihanna?" he asked.

He always seemed to know what to ask when I was at a loss for words.

"Photography."

We both perked up. "Really. That's great. Is that what you want to study in college?" I asked.

I had no idea if she even planned to go.

"I want to be a photojournalist. On the way from the bathroom, I noticed what you would call a suspect board."

Whoops. We should have taken that down. "Yes. I don't

know if you saw the sign outside, but Jaxson and I run The Pink Iguana Sleuth Agency."

"Cool. Do you investigate whether some guy is cheating on his wife or something?"

"We could, but so far, we seemed to get mixed up in murders."

"Here? In sleepy Witch's Cove?"

I took offense at the sleepy part. That implied we were backward. I suppose, compared to Jacksonville—our largest Florida city—we were. "We have had our share."

"Awesome." She turned to Jaxson. "Have you ever shot anyone?"

"I don't carry a gun."

"Oh. Well, if you ever need help with any of your cases, let me know. I'd love to write about your adventures."

As great as it would be to have someone journal our investigations—mostly so that we could refer back to what people told us—that wasn't what I wanted my young cousin to be doing.

"I'll keep that in mind."

Someone knocked. The door opened, and Steve poked his head in. "Oh, I'm sorry. I didn't know you had company."

"It's okay," I said. "Come in."

He'd met my mom. It would be good if he was aware that my cousin was an underage relative. If he caught her roaming where she shouldn't, I wanted him to let me know. I introduced him to Rihanna.

Naturally, Rihanna seemed smitten. I figured she'd be difficult, but not because she'd swoon every time she saw a good looking man.

Rihanna scooted over, and Steve sat next to her. "I wanted to say thank you for convincing Trevor to turn himself in," the sheriff said.

"He turned himself in? For what?"

"For hitting his father."

"I never told him to do any such thing. His dad was alive after their altercation." My blood pressure shot up.

Steve held up his hand. "Don't worry. He's not being charged. Trevor stopped in and mentioned that he and his father had a difference of opinion about Trevor's goals."

"And you believed him?" I asked.

"I'm not that judgmental, especially after he showed me his bruised ribs. While anyone could have punched him, his story of what happened to his father matched perfectly to the crime scene and medical examiner's report."

"I don't understand," Jaxson said.

"Like he told you, Trevor's father hit him, and Trevor responded with a facial punch, only his dad ducked."

I finished the sentence. "And Trevor's blow hit his father's temple instead."

"Yes. Trevor left his dad's office right after that. I called Mr. Merriman's doctor about what effect a blow like that could have on a man his age. Turns out Mr. Merriman was on medication for low blood pressure, because he often had fainting spells."

"Mrs. Merriman mentioned that," I said, but I couldn't be sure if I told the sheriff that fact or not.

"When I contacted Mrs. Merriman, she told me that her husband hadn't been taking the pills recently."

"What does that mean?" Jaxson asked.

"It's hard to say exactly. The blow to the head might have caused some internal bleeding. After Trevor left, Mr. Merriman probably stood up too fast. He walked around to the front of his desk and suddenly felt faint. For support, he grabbed the desk."

I looked over at Jaxson. "Don't tell me, he knocked off the award, then hit his head on the desk, and bled out?"

"That's what we're thinking. His back would have been to the desk since we found his blood on the corner."

I really needed to learn more about the law. "If Trevor's blow caused it, is he responsible for his father's death?"

"No, because in this case it was self-defense. His father hit first, or so Trevor says, and we have no reason to believe otherwise."

I needed a moment to absorb this. "Does that mean no one murdered Mr. Merriman?"

"That's our conclusions. It was an unfortunate accident in which Mr. Merriman's anger and stubborn refusal to take medication caused his death."

"I guess Mrs. Merriman was only partially psychic."

"How so?" Steve asked.

"She had a feeling her husband would die, but she got the location wrong. I've heard that often happens with dreams. It's all a matter of interpretation."

"Good to know."

"How is Trevor holding up?" I asked.

A small smile crossed Steve's lips. He looked over at my mother. "It was the message you received from Mr. Merriman—the deceased—that seemed to give Trevor solace. After I explained what I believed happened, the message became clear."

"Did it mean that it was Mr. Merriman's fault for getting angry?"

"We believe so."

Wow. I didn't see that coming. "I guess that case is closed. For real this time." One down, one to go.

Steve stood. "Yes, but I have a favor to ask."

"Sure."

"Considering you talk to everyone, I'm sure Trevor would appreciate it if you only mentioned that Mr. Merriman passed out, hit his head, and died. There doesn't need to be any mention of the fight with his son. In fact, that blow might not have caused anything. It's only speculation that it could have, and we all know how this town can blow things out of proportion."

What a wonderful gesture on Steve's part. "My lips are sealed, and thank you. I know Trevor will appreciate it."

Steve left, and I was suddenly lighter.

"Wow," Rihanna said.

I probably should have asked her to go into her room. She didn't need to be exposed to such sordid details, but she'd already seen our suspect board. I wanted to create a distraction and held up my iced tea. "This calls for a celebration."

All four of us tapped our glasses. I didn't think that this day could have gone any better.

Just as I relaxed, Penny rushed in. "I'm glad I caught you." She stopped. "Oh. I didn't know you had company."

I suppose having guests in our place of business was not such a good idea. "Penny, this is Rihanna, my cousin I told you about."

Perky Penny bounced over and shook her hand. "Nice to meet you."

"You, too."

I was happy my aunt had taught her some manners.

Penny spun around. "You won't guess what Hunter and I found last night."

"What?"

She slipped next to Rihanna on the sofa as that was the only available seat. I could only hope that Sassy hadn't suddenly taken up residence on that spot.

"Hunter and I decided to get some ice cream last night, and you will never believe what we found."

"What is that?"

"A Barbados Nut tree."

The calm that had claimed my body disappeared. "Where?"

"In front of the ice cream shop. We've seen it a hundred times but never knew what it was."

"Why does anyone care?" Rihanna asked.

If her question hadn't sounded so sincere, I might have dismissed it. I suppose it wouldn't hurt to bring her up to speed just in case she wanted to spend her days writing her story. "Another man was murdered a day before Mr. Merriman died. His name was Chester Hightower."

"Why him?" she asked.

I gave her a brief rundown of his desire to keep his theater from being torn down and turned into a condo, and the request by Mr. Merriman to buy it as well as the ice cream shop. "Everyone wanted the condo to go forward but Mr. Hightower."

"You think someone killed him so they wouldn't have any more opposition?"

She caught on quickly. "Yes."

"I know what you're going to say," Penny said. "We have no idea if Mr. Plimpton cut any of the branches in order to gather the nuts. Even if he did, you don't know if he then gave them to Mr. Hightower. Though Hunter did a quick scan and said some of the branches had been recently severed. I agree it could be someone wanting to prune the tree."

I loved it when Penny got into the crime solving business with me.

Iggy hopped up on the coffee table. "Sassy wants me to tell you that Mr. Hightower always complained about how Mr. Plimpton never took care of the landscaping in front of his place. Her owner did it."

"Tell Sassy thank you."

"Who's Sassy?" Rihanna asked.

"Iggy, why don't you tell my cousin who she is."

Iggy faced her. "Sassy is a cat ghost who was Mr. Hightower's pet at one time."

Rihanna's mouth opened. "You can really talk to ghosts?

Iggy puffed out his chest. Oh, boy. "Yes. I'm special like that. Only I can see and talk to her."

Just yesterday, he'd considered it a curse.

"That is way cool." She sobered. "Where does Mr. Plimpton live?"

"I don't know," I quickly said, even though I'd already looked up his home address. "I hope you aren't thinking about investigating." Photojournalist or not.

"Of course not."

I relaxed. "Good."

Penny had probably just finished her shift and needed to pick up Tommy. "Thanks for finding the tree. I'll think of a way to find out if Mr. Plimpton was involved in any way. He is old, so maybe he never knew those nuts were harmful."

Penny stood. "If you need me or Hunter to help in any other way, let me know."

"Will do."

After she said goodbye to the others, she left.

"Will you guys excuse me?" Rihanna said. "I'd like to unpack."

"Sure," I said, curious what her abrupt departure was about.

Teenagers. I'd never understand them.

## CHAPTER 15

Because Mr. Merriman's death had been resolved, and there really wasn't much to do about Mr. Hightower's demise, I thought I would sleep in. I had shown Rihanna where the Tiki Hut Grill was and told her that she could eat there for free. Just to be clear, I instructed Aunt Fern to put Rihanna's bill on my tab, but she wouldn't hear of it. Rihanna was her relative too—by marriage, but still.

And then there was Iggy. He insisted on staying with my cousin, just in case she needed a man around. I did love his protective streak, but I had the sense he was still angry with me for not agreeing to let him get his tail pierced.

I had asked about Sassy being in the office, but Iggy said that since she wasn't constrained by walls, the cat ghost would follow him wherever he went. I'd used that argument with him before, but only now did he apparently agree with me.

To be honest, I was more relaxed knowing Iggy could rush out and wake me should Rihanna need something.

Because my body liked to betray me, I awoke around eight the next morning, and it refused to let me fall back asleep. I eventually gave up and got out of bed. After I fixed myself a bowl of cereal and poured a cup of coffee, I sat at the kitchen table and looked out at the beach. Even though I'd lived in Witch's Cove all of my life, except when I went to college and taught for a year, I didn't take advantage of the beach as much as I should have. Maybe now that Rihanna was here, it would be something we could do together.

Before I headed to work, I did a little cleaning around my apartment. When I entered the office, Iggy and Aimee were in the corner chatting, and the exchange seemed amicable, thank goodness.

*Thank you, Jaxson, for installing the cat door!*

"Aimee, when did you get here?" I asked. It was early, though I suppose animals didn't sleep like we did.

"Last night after you came home. I was worried about Iggy, so I thought I'd check to see if he was here."

She never came into the apartment and asked where he was. I bet Iggy wanted to get rid of me last night so he could have a sleepover. "Iggy, you can have Aimee over any time you want. You don't need to pull a con to do it."

"I know, but it was easier not to tell you. Besides, this gives us more privacy when you're not around."

"Whatever." When had he grown up? I looked around. "Is Rihanna still in bed?"

"No," Iggy said. "She said she wanted to take some sunrise pictures. She left a while ago with all of her camera gear."

I stepped over to the window and looked out. It was possible she was the lone person far down the beach with the seagulls surrounding her, but I couldn't be sure.

I was happy knowing that she had found something she was passionate about. These next few months might not be as stressful as I thought they'd be. Since she mentioned she liked the town's architecture, maybe she was taking pictures of scenic Witch's Cove.

Before I could ponder where she was, Jaxson emerged from the inner stairwell. He was sporting his usual pink silicone wrist band, but he now had on his black Pink Iguana Sleuth t-shirt. I bet Rihanna would like his choice of color.

"Sorry, I'm late. I stopped by Darren Hightower's office."

"What for?"

"I mentioned that the tree next to his establishment was a Barbados Nut tree, and I thought it was possible his father had picked some of the nuts and eaten them."

"What a great catch. What did he say?"

"His dad never would have done that. He considered all unknown things to be dangerous. One time, Darren, his father, and his late brother, Tim, went camping in the Appalachian foothills of northern Georgia. There were berry bushes everywhere. While Tim was certain nothing was poisonous, his dad said not to eat them. He was extremely cautious when it came to eating fruit or mushrooms, unless it was deemed safe by an expert."

"I can see his point. I'm always leery of mushrooms. And snakes. And a lot of other things. Once I know they are harmless, though, I'm good."

He smiled. "I also asked if he hired a gardener to trim the tree."

"And?"

"No, he did not. That means either cheapskate Plimpton did it himself, or he found the cash to hire someone."

"Maybe we should ask him," I suggested.

"I'm one step ahead of you. I stopped by the ice cream shop, but it wasn't open yet."

"Maybe you can stop by later?"

"I intend to. Anyway, no gardener worth his salt would have cut off a few limbs without trimming the other ones. Not only that, the hedge in front is full of weeds."

"Interesting."

Jaxson looked around. "Where's Rihanna?"

"Out taking pictures."

"She must be serious about being a photojournalist."

"So it seems." He stepped over to his desk. "What's our next step with the Hightower case, besides trying to figure out if Plimpton fed the nuts to Chester?"

"What do you think about us having an early lunch at the diner? Dolly probably has a few tidbits to share about Mr. Plimpton."

"I love the way you think."

"Thanks. Now that Rihanna is here, I probably need to do a little straightening up around the office. How about giving me an hour?"

"Perfect."

To my delight, Rihanna had made her bed and put away her clothes. I chuckled. Her closet looked like mine—monochromatic. I had to give her props for standing up for her individuality. I'm sure it couldn't have been easy.

I had no idea if she'd gone to the Tiki Hut for breakfast. If not, she'd be hungry at some point. I also didn't know if she had any cash on her. I didn't have a lot to spare, but I could give her some mad money. If Jaxson or I needed some sit-in-your-car type of surveillance, we might pay her to do that boring job—at least until school started. She had her own car, so she wouldn't have to borrow mine.

That reminded me that we'd have to take a trip to school to get her registered for senior year. I know that Mom should have been the one—being her aunt and all—but she's been so distracted of late that I didn't want to add another burden. Besides, I'd know which teachers to recommend.

Today though, I'd let Rihanna enjoy what Witch's Cove had to offer.

After I left my cousin a note to help herself to anything in the refrigerator, I joined Jaxson in the main room. "Ready for some gossip?"

"Absolutely. If you can't talk to the person of interest, the gossip queens are the next best thing—and safer, too. I'm surprised you don't pick your Aunt's brain more often."

I experienced some guilt over that. "I know, but then she'd lecture me about how dangerous it could be chasing after a murderer."

"She'd be right," Jaxson said.

"I know. Someone killed Mr. Hightower, and for all we know, Darren did it."

"I'm sure Steve checked his alibi."

"He did, but Darren said he was with Amanda at the time of his dad's death."

"Are you buying that?" Jaxson asked.

"Honestly, no."

He smiled. "Good. I don't want you to get soft on me."

I laughed. As we headed over to the diner, I looked around the streets, trying to spot Rihanna. Either she was at the beach or far down the street shooting our vintage town. Though if she spotted the Hex and Bones Apothecary, she would have a heyday taking pictures in there.

As soon as we stepped into the diner, I spotted Dolly and waved. I needed to talk to Jaxson about making her an honorary member of our amateur sleuth company. She always was good for some gossip.

We grabbed a booth. Before she came over, I checked out the menu. Chocolate chip pancakes with whipped cream would really hit the spot. Who cared if it was lunchtime?

"You guys are becoming regulars," Dolly said. "I like it."

"Let's order first, and then we'd like to pick your brain."

"My favorite thing to do—gossip." She smiled and then pulled out her pad.

I ordered my sugar-laden meal while Jaxson had scrambled eggs, bacon, and fruit.

Dolly put in the order and then returned. She slipped into the booth next to Jaxson. "What's new?"

"The Merriman case is closed," I said, wanting to make sure she'd heard.

"Pearl called and filled me in."

I told her my belief that Mr. Hightower had died from nut poisoning. "Penny and Hunter noticed a Barbados Nut tree in front of the ice cream shop."

"You don't say."

She sounded genuinely surprised. "What's even more odd is that some of the branches have been cut."

"Who would do that?"

"We don't know, but what about Mr. Plimpton? What do you know about him?"

"Gerald? Why he's a sweet man. Ever since his wife died about three years ago, he hasn't been the same. The two of them came in here all the time. After she passed, he's kind of kept to himself."

"Since he agreed to sell his ice cream shop to Mr. Merriman, and then Mr. Hightower said he wouldn't sell, it put a kibosh on that development. Mr. Plimpton might be upset over that."

"Possibly. I'd heard he's pretty desperate to leave town. His grandson in Connecticut is ill, and he wants to be with him."

That was sad. "And Mr. Plimpton may not have all that many years left either."

"Right." Her cell rang, and even I recognized the ring. It was Pearl.

"Go ahead and answer it," I said.

"Pearl?" She listened for a bit. "Amanda's fingerprints? Did Steve arrest her?"

My heart raced, and even Jaxson was leaning in close,

probably trying to hear. A while ago, I had put a spell on him that gave him super eyesight and super hearing—like that of the werewolves we'd uncovered in the forest. Unfortunately, the spell had worn off. From what I'd heard, repeated spells close together might cause harm, so I never asked him to do it again. Thankfully, his ability to communicate with Iggy remained intact.

Dolly hung up. "I guess you heard."

"Only some of it," I said.

"You know the death threat that Mr. Hightower received?"

"Sure."

"Steve finally got the lab results back. It had Amanda's fingerprints on it."

"He had her prints on file?" Jaxson asked.

"Yes, from when she worked in the county tax office many years ago."

Whoa. "Did she confess to killing her father-in-law?" It seemed like I had to drag the information out of her.

"No. She said she had an alibi for when he was killed."

That again? "I hardly think Darren should count as her alibi. They could have killed him together."

"She told Steve she lied about that. The truth was she was at the spa getting her nails done during the time of her father-in-law's death."

"Why not say that in the first place?" Jaxson asked.

"Pearl couldn't hear the rest of the conversation."

"I'll ask Priscilla," I said. "I've seen Amanda in the nail salon a time or two."

That seemed like a long time ago—when I had money to spare. Now I only had my nails done when I needed some gossip from the owner.

"That's great. Talk to her," Dolly said. "But be sure to call me afterward. Quid Pro Quo and all."

I had no problem with that. "Deal."

Dolly left to get our food. "If I visit Priscilla, what will you do?"

Jaxson huffed. "I might go back and talk to Darren. Ask him why he lied about being with Amanda during his father's death."

"That could be dangerous, especially if he's the killer. Besides, I'm sure Steve will talk to him."

Jaxson shrugged. "I'm not worried about Darren. I can take him."

Men and their macho attitudes. "What if he pulls a gun on you?"

Jaxson reached across the table and clasped my hand. "Are you worried about me, pink lady?"

"Yes, of course I am. Who would I get to do all my research if you're dead?"

Jax let go of my hand and slapped it over his heart. "You wound me."

I had to laugh. It didn't matter how stressful my day was, Jaxson always made me smile.

Our food arrived, breaking our connection for the moment. My breakfast choice had been outstanding, and I scarfed down my meal in no time. To Jaxson's credit, he didn't comment on my choice of food.

When we were done, I waved for the server and handed her my credit card.

"Let me see your nails," Jaxson said.

I held out my hands. "Three are chipped. Priscilla will so believe that I need a manicure."

"Good luck."

"You, too. If Darren seems edgy for any reason, let Steve know."

"I got this," Jax said.

And I believed he did.

## CHAPTER 16

Since the nail salon was just down the street, I chose to walk instead of drive. As I was about to pull open the entry door, who should be exiting but none other than Sheriff Steve Rocker.

"Glinda? What are you doing here?"

I don't know why he acted so surprised. "What? A girl can't get her nails done in this town?"

"Seriously? I can read you like a book. Somehow you found out about the fingerprints on the death threat, didn't you?"

"I don't know what you're talking about." I saw no reason to confess.

"Let me see your hands." He wiggled his fingers for me to show him my nails.

He was right about my purpose, but he couldn't dispute the sad state of my manicure. I hadn't had one since I was trying to pump Priscilla for information about our dead bowling alley man. I showed him my nails. "See?"

"Hmm. You're right, but I still don't believe you." He tipped two fingers to his forehead and strode off.

Phew. That was close, but he didn't have to look almost horrified at the state of my polish. It wasn't like I had totally neglected my appearance. It was only a couple of chipped nails, one broken one, and one mangled cuticle. Who knew Steve Rocker was such a nail expert?

I went inside and breathed a sigh of relief that the place wasn't crowded. As luck would have it, Priscilla, the owner, was manning the desk.

"Glinda. This is a nice surprise. Did you see the hunky sheriff on the way in?"

"I did. What did he want?" As if I didn't know.

"He needed to know if someone's alibi was true."

And? She said nothing. Darn. I wished she had spilled the beans right away. This gossip session might be more difficult than I thought. "Was it true?"

"Yes."

I showed her my nails. "Can you give me a quick polish?"

"Sure. Follow me."

After seeing my cousin dress only in black, I could see how I must look to others. "I want to try something different today," I said.

"I love it."

After I told her my plan, I relaxed in the chair. "You don't have to tell me if you don't want, but I'm guessing the person needing an alibi was Amanda Hightower. Am I right?"

No surprise, her eyes widened. "Did the sheriff mention that?"

She probably wanted to see if it was okay to say more. "More or less."

"Yes, it was Amanda."

Steve never confided in me regarding the time of Mr. Hightower's death. Even if I guessed that he died within two hours of me leaving his house, that would mean Amanda had to have been at the spa for quite some time in order to provide a good alibi. "What did she have done? Was it the complete spa package?" I would love to do that someday.

Priscilla smiled. "Yup. The whole shebang."

I couldn't fathom how much that would cost. "I thought she was hurting for money."

Priscilla lifted my hands out of the solution and removed the polish on my right hand. "She was until she sold a piece of jewelry her husband had given her. Amanda said it was too painful to look at it every day. From what she implied, that sale would tide her over financially for some time."

I whistled. "That must have been some piece of jewelry."

"It had to have been."

I could understand why she'd sell something that personal. Even though I wore my magic crystal around my neck, every time I touched it, I was reminded of my grandmother, and that brought me a combination of both joy and sorrow.

"I thought she said she was with Darren at the time of Mr. Hightower's death." By now, the whole town would have learned the details.

"She only said that to protect Darren's secret."

Secret? "You mean the fact he and Olivia were an item?" Or that he killed his dad?

"Yes. The two of them were together at the time."

That wasn't the juicy tidbit I would have liked, but the truth was the truth. Since I'd learned what I wanted, we chatted about the bowling league that had come to a halt after one of its members had been killed right on the alley. Priscilla had no idea that his death had been about a power struggle in the werewolf clan, and I certainly wasn't going to enlighten her.

Once I finished, I was anxious to fill Jaxson in on what I'd learned. I also wanted to show Rihanna my new nails.

On my walk home, I called Dolly to let her know Amanda had told the truth.

"She couldn't have murdered Chester then," Dolly said.

"Nope."

"Thanks for letting me know."

Happy to have paid back some gossip, I returned to the office. When I entered, I expected my cousin to be there watching television or reading a book. It was what I used to do as a kid. Only she wasn't there. Jaxson was, however. Good enough.

"How did your spa day go?" he asked.

"I just got my nails done." I walked over to him and wiggled my fingers. I was rather proud of my progress.

He looked down at my nails and then up at me. "Who are you, and what have you done with Glinda, the lady who only wears pink?"

I laughed. When I had to sneak through the woods one time to find some werewolves, Penny dressed me up in all black. I realized then that I could break out of my pink mold if need be. "I wanted to honor Rihanna. My nails are still pink. They just have black tips."

"I, for one, like them. Makes you edgier."

"Edgier? Did I need more edge?" I'm not sure if I liked that.

"I like you both ways. First, tell me what Priscilla said, and then I'll share my news."

I explained about seeing Sheriff Rocker leaving the spa, and that I had to prove to him that I really was there to get my nails done.

Jaxson fought a smile. "He knows you well."

"Yes, but it wasn't like he could stop me from going in."

"Continue."

I told him about Amanda selling some jewelry to partially

pay for her spa day. "What she had done would take her hours."

"This means she didn't kill her father-in-law."

"Correct."

"We should remove her name from our suspect board then, assuming we believe she didn't hire anyone to kill her father-in-law."

"I don't believe she did, but I could be wrong. What did you find out about Darren?" I asked.

"He admitted to lying. Of course, he wasn't with Amanda but rather Olivia. Their relationship was still private at that point since Mr. Merriman was alive, or at least Darren wasn't aware he'd died."

"That's exactly what Priscilla told me, too."

"Good to know," he said.

I suppose we should ask Olivia to corroborate his story, but she'd only lie for Darren Hightower if need be. I looked at the wall clock. "Have you seen Rihanna?"

"No."

As if I could conjure up a person by asking about them, the door opened, and my cousin rushed in. Her face was flushed, and she was a little out of breath. I was a bit surprised at her attire—rather short black shorts and a skimpy black tank top. The black combat boots were a nice touch though. It was a far cry from the baggy jeans and oversized shirt she'd drove down in yesterday. Instead of a ponytail, her hair was braided, probably to keep from getting in her way when she took photos.

"You guys won't believe what I saw."

I'd never seen her so excited. "Do tell."

She motioned that we draw up our chairs around her. "Okay, a little background. When I left this morning, I wanted to capture the sunrise and then explore Witch's Cove

—which, by the way, I did. It was so cool, and the town is really quaint."

"Many photographers come here to capture the unique architecture of the town as well as the beauty of the beaches. Just wait until you see some of our sunsets. They are incredible, too."

"I can't wait, though I did get a lot of great shots already. Needing a break from the heat, I decided to stop at the ice cream shop to see what all the fuss was about."

My muscles tensed. I hope she wanted to understand what Jaxson and I were working on and nothing more. "It's a little rundown, I admit, but it has a lot of fond memories," I said.

"I loved it. It has so much character."

My heart swelled. Hearing it from a visitor—even if she happened to be a relative—meant a lot to me. "I'm glad you had a good day."

"I did." Rihanna happened to glance at my nails as I was brushing back my hair.

"Is that black I see?" Rihanna asked with excitement in her voice.

I held out my hands. "This is the first touch of black that has ever graced my nails. It's in honor of you. If you were able to sleep with pink sheets and a pink bedspread, I could bend a little and have a touch of black."

"That's great, cuz."

I laughed. Even though we were only nine years apart, I considered her a kid. "But don't think I'm wearing a black headband or anything."

"Definitely not, just like I'm not wearing a pink t-shirt."

"Deal," I said.

Her eyes widened. "I haven't told you the best part of my day. I was sitting outside eating my sundae when this old guy walks out of the shop. He had the best face."

I didn't think kids appreciated age. "Why is that?"

"He had a gnarly mustache." She chuckled. "And eyebrows that stuck out like he'd put his finger in a socket." She demonstrated with the backs of her hands on her own brows and wiggled her fingers.

"Can you show us a picture of him?" Jaxson asked.

"Sure." She pulled up the photo on her DSLR. When she turned the camera around, I sucked in a breath.

"That's Mr. Plimpton. The owner of the shop."

Rihanna's mouth opened. "You've got to be kidding. It makes sense now."

Not to me, it didn't. "What do you mean?"

"Okay, so I was sitting there, and the old guy—I mean, Mr. Plimpton—sat at one of the tables, but he wasn't eating anything. It was like he was waiting for someone."

I didn't remember ever being this excited over a person sitting at a table before, but I was happy Rihanna found it intriguing. "Then what?"

"I took some selfies with my phone, and then switched it to the other direction and shot some of him. He had no clue what I was doing, but here's the good part. A guy comes out of the theater and calls the old guy over."

That could have been Darren Hightower. The theater was closed. "How old was he?"

She shrugged. "I'd say Uncle Stan's age."

Dad was fifty. "Did you take a picture of him too?"

"Sure did." She pulled it up and showed it to us.

"That's Darren Hightower."

Rihanna pumped a fist. "I knew it."

"Why is that?" Jaxson asked.

"Because when the two got together, the old guy started yelling at Mr. Hightower, saying that he'd promised to sell, and he can't go back on his word now."

I looked over at Jaxson. "That puts a new spin on things," I said.

Jaxson turned back to Rihanna. "Are you sure that is what he said?"

"Yes. Here. I recorded it all."

She was amazing. Together, the three of us watched the video. It was unbelievable.

"That's it," she said. "Then they left."

"You are destined to be a great snoop," I said, and I meant it too.

"Thanks."

"We need to take that to the sheriff," Jaxson said.

I thought that too. "Plimpton never confessed he had anything to do with Mr. Hightower's death, just that he was mad now that Darren had decided not to sell."

"True, but it might point Steve in the right direction. Do we know if the sheriff even questioned Mr. Plimpton about Hightower's death?"

"I have no idea," I said.

"I can take it to him," Rihanna said with a glint in her eye.

"That is so sweet of you to offer, but I think Jaxson and I should do it. Rest assured, we'll give you all the credit. Can you download that file and put it on a flash drive?"

"Sure. Be right back."

Gotta love kids these days. She was quite tech savvy. "What do you think?" I asked Jaxson.

"About your cousin or the video?"

"Both."

"She's street smart, gutsy, and resourceful. As for the video, it might help show Steve that Mr. Plimpton is no saint."

"That was what I was thinking. Plimpton was mad, sure, but I'm having a hard time believing he would poison his friend."

"You heard him. He already put his house up for sale. He wants to leave town and be with his family up north."

"I know," I said. It was hard for me to think ill of people I'd known since I was a kid.

Rihanna came out of her bedroom and handed us the flash drive. "Here you go."

"Thank you." I stood. "Jax and I won't be long."

"Don't worry about me. I'm going to grab a bite to eat and head on out."

"Aren't you tired? The pictures will be there tomorrow."

"Thanks, but I'm good. I'll be starting school soon, and I want to take advantage of the time I have."

She sure did have a great attitude. In all honesty, I didn't recall any of my high school friends being so mature, unless she had other plans. Hmm. "Okay. You can take Iggy if you want."

Iggy spun around in circles. "Please," he begged.

"Next time, buddy, okay?"

He dropped down onto his stomach. "Okay."

I didn't blame her. Iggy could be a handful at times.

Jax and I left with the flash drive and headed across the street to the sheriff's office. "This should garner you some brownie points," Jaxson said.

"I'm not doing it for that. I want the killer caught, one way or the other."

He held up a palm. "Me, too."

Jennifer Larsen was at the desk instead of Pearl, and thankfully, both Steve and Nash were there. Since Steve was lead on this case, I asked to talk to him. "We have some evidence in the Hightower murder." I waved the drive.

"Oh. Go on back. I'm sure you know the way."

That was a bit snarky. "I do."

We found Steve at his desk reading from one of his

yellow note pads. He looked up. "Glinda. Jaxson. What can I do for you?"

I handed him the flash drive. "My cousin, Rihanna, was enjoying an ice cream sundae when an argument broke out between Mr. Plimpton and Darren Hightower. Wanting to be a photojournalist, she recorded the whole thing."

He whistled. "I take it there are some interesting pieces of information in here?" he asked as he plugged it into his computer.

"Not a confession exactly, but close."

"Have a seat, and let's take a look."

## CHAPTER 17

The sheriff had to turn up the volume on the recording since the wind noise made it difficult to hear everything. Mr. Plimpton's arm waving and shouts implied he was not a happy camper.

"I talked to Olivia Merriman, and she said her dad's company would buy my place," Mr. Plimpton said, leaning a bit too close to Darren Hightower.

"Sure, if and only if, dad agreed to sell the theater, which he didn't."

Plimpton stepped back and dragged a hand down his mustache. "He was never going to agree, and you and I both know it. It's why something had to be done. Stubborn old coot. You even said he was losing money and had to take out loans to keep the place afloat."

"That's all true, but Dad would have come around. Eventually. Even though he paid on time, the banks told him no more loans."

Mr. Plimpton stilled. "I didn't know that. Regardless, he's gone, and my grandson is sick. I can't wait any longer." His anger and frustration radiated off him. "I have to sell and get away from this town." More arm waving.

Darren moved closer. "Did you do something to my father?"

*"Me? No! But now that the old coot is dead, I want to re-negotiate. We can go back to the Merrimans and see if the offer stills stands. The company is alive. His kids are now in charge."*

*Darren huffed out a breath. "Here's the thing. Now that Olivia's dad is out of the picture, she and I can finally marry. She loves the theater as much as my dad does—or rather did. She wants to help restore it."*

*Mr. Plimpton's hands fisted. "Does that mean you're going back on your word?"*

*Darren stood taller. "I guess it does, but I'll tell you what I'll do. I think Olivia may buy you out anyway. She mentioned that we could put a door between the theater and your shop. Make it one place. See a movie and then go for ice cream."*

*Plimpton shook his head. "Well, you better hurry up and do something fast. Or else."*

*"Is that a threat?" Darren asked, his eyes narrowing.*

*"Take it any way you want."*

The video ended, and the sheriff blew out a breath. "I agree there's no admission of guilt, but that is one angry store owner."

"Honestly, I don't blame him. Mr. Plimpton was counting on selling his place, and then Darren does a one-eighty," I said.

"True. Too many times, though, I've seen desperate men do dumb things," the sheriff responded.

I held up a finger. "There's something else."

"What's that?" Steve asked.

"You mentioned that the medical examiner believed Mr. Hightower might have been poisoned, right?"

"Yes, and you thought the same thing," Steve said.

"I did. While we don't know which poison it was, Hunter Ashwell spotted a Barbados Nut tree in front of the ice cream shop with some of the limbs cut. Barbados nuts can be poisonous."

I wondered if Steve would draw the same conclusion I had. "Are you saying, you think Plimpton picked the nuts and gave them to Chester Hightower in the hopes that the old man would eat them and die?"

"It's a good theory," I said.

Jaxson leaned forward. "What would you do if you were old man Plimpton? You are offered the chance of a lifetime to dump the albatross that has been keeping you here for years. Now that your grandson is sick, you have the chance to return to your family. Plimpton is an old, lonely man, nearing the end of his life, and the only impediment to realizing his dream is another old man."

Steve nodded. "I get it. He has motive. Apparently, Mr. Plimpton had opportunity too, but that doesn't mean he killed Chester Hightower."

To be fair, I needed to shed some light. "Even if Mr. Plimpton admitted to giving Mr. Hightower the nuts, some say these nuts have medicinal benefits. Plimpton might not have known they could be lethal."

"I see. Amanda admitted to writing the death threat, but that's all. We can't tie Plimpton to any of this. And since we have no proof, we can't arrest him," Steve said.

"Right, and even if Amanda and Mr. Plimpton were in this together—she writes the note and Mr. Plimpton delivers the nuts—she'd never admit it."

"True," Steve said. "Short of a confession, I got nothing."

That wasn't good, but he was the sheriff. "Are you giving up?" I asked.

"No. If Plimpton is guilty, he'll slip up sooner or later."

"We can only hope."

Steve pulled out the flash drive after saving its contents. "Thank Rihanna for this. It could be critical to cracking this case."

"I will."

After we left, we headed back to the office. Even though we—and Rihanna—tried to solve the case, an unsettled feeling of malaise settled in my gut. I wanted to do more research or something, but we'd run out of people to talk to.

Rihanna was playing with Iggy when we came in. "I thought you said you were going out again to take pictures."

"I changed my mind. I was more tired than I thought."

"I trust no one stopped by?" I could only hope.

"Nope."

"Since it's still fairly early, do you want to stop by the high school and sign up for classes?"

She scrunched up her nose. "No, but I guess I can't avoid the inevitable."

While we were speaking with the sheriff, instead of going out, she'd showered and changed. Her black jeans and slogan-less t-shirt didn't even have any holes in either of them. "Great." I turned to Jaxson. "We shouldn't be long."

Once at the high school, we were escorted into the admission director's office. I explained the circumstances of Rihanna's new living arrangements, and the counselor was very sympathetic.

"There will be some work you'll need to do for the start of school." She explained what needed to be done.

"Great." Rihanna's lack of enthusiasm came as no surprise. I wouldn't have wanted to read two books and do a summer project in less than two weeks, but it would keep her busy.

"As for which classes to take, what are you interested in?" the counselor asked. "Each student gets one extracurricular class."

"I'm going to be a photojournalist," Rihanna announced with certainty.

"That's great. You didn't happen to bring any of your work with you, did you?"

I probably should have thought to suggest it. Oh, well.

"Yes, I did."

Okay, never mind.

Rihanna pulled out four images. I was happy to see our new color printer was getting some use. I couldn't see which ones she handed to Mrs. Carmichael, but I'm sure they had something to do with Witch's Cove.

The guidance counselor studied them. "These are really good. I especially love the one of the old man."

"Thanks. I'm thinking about asking him if I can do a photo shoot. His hands show years of experience."

Mrs. Carmichael smiled while I wanted to scream that the man might be a murderer. If not, he'd love the attention and company.

She handed the photos back to Rihanna. "You have a lot of potential. How about doing a photo essay on this man?"

I had to work hard to keep from saying no in front of the counselor. I'm sure we could find another suitable person to showcase. I searched my brain for someone as interesting, but came up empty—for now.

After Rihanna picked her classes, the counselor gave her a guided tour, and my high school memories came flooding back—some good, some not. "Is Mrs. Henderson still teaching English?" I asked. That class made me shiver.

"Oh, yes. She's an icon at this school."

More like a relic. To Rihanna's credit, she didn't make any snarky comments. When the tour ended, we thanked the counselor and left.

"You do realize you can't actually interview Mr. Plimpton, right?" I asked the moment we were outside.

"Why not? He's not going to kill me. It wouldn't serve his purpose."

Wow, that was an optimistic attitude and a bit naive. "He might kidnap you and use you as leverage somehow."

"You're just being paranoid. He doesn't know I'm your cousin."

She might have a point, though I didn't like being labeled as someone who was obsessively anxious. "We'll find someone else. Don't you worry."

"Sure."

I didn't buy her concession for a minute. Once at the office, Rihanna went to her room. She claimed she had to download some of the books and start reading. Her proactive attitude really impressed me, though my sixth sense told me something else was going on.

I returned to the main room. "How did it go?" Jaxson asked.

I told him about Rihanna's assignment. As expected, his brows furrowed. "I suggested she pick someone else, but she isn't hearing it."

"We'll give her some alternatives," Jaxson said.

"She seems to like the wrinkly old person type." Of course. "I bet she'd love Gertrude Poole."

"Yes. She's perfect."

That was easy. "Tomorrow, I'll take Rihanna over to the Psychics Corner and introduce them. In the meantime, do we know anything more about Gerald Plimpton?"

"He did put his house up for sale, and from the social media sites, his grandson is very ill. He's telling the truth about that."

"I'm sorry to hear that. Did you find out the property value of his shop?"

"Yes. The tax records show its value, but sad to say, every few years, its value has been deteriorating."

"That implies he really might be desperate. But enough to kill an old friend? I mean they've been business neighbors for a long time."

Jaxson nodded. "You would think friendship would trump money, but that's not always the case."

Since there was basically nothing more for me to do, and Rihanna seemed determined to hole up in her room, I thought I'd visit my aunt. "I'm going to touch base with Aunt Fern."

"Because?"

I chuckled. "Because I haven't seen her in a while. We need to catch up."

Jaxson waved a hand. "You go. I'll make sure our resident teenager is taken care of."

He was the best. "Thank you. I'll see you tomorrow morning then. Do you have plans for the evening?"

"Just more research."

"Don't work too hard." I looked over at Iggy. "Do you want to come with me?"

"I think I should stay here. Rihanna and I have nice chats at night."

Surprisingly, I wasn't jealous. I loved that Iggy cared about my cousin. If he was chatting with Rihanna, maybe Sassy wouldn't bother him. Who knows?

When I entered the Tiki Hut Grill, Aunt Fern was not at the counter, which meant she probably was upstairs in her apartment, though she had been known to grab a tea or coffee at either Maude's or Miriam's place. She must derive a lot of comfort knowing her friends had her back.

When I reached the landing, I heard her chatting with Aimee. Having a cat—especially one who could answer back —had been a boost to her morale. I really had thought when she agreed to start dating that her life would turn around, but the first guy she went out with ended up being a male chauvinist who didn't appreciate Aunt Fern's quirky characteristics.

I knocked on her door, and she answered quickly. "Glinda, what a nice surprise."

*That was code for you've been ignoring me.* "I thought we could catch up."

"Come in."

Aimee pranced up to me. "I'll make sure Iggy isn't lonely."

"He's not, or are you still jealous because of Sassy?"

"Whatever do you mean?"

I didn't have time to debate with a cat. "Jaxson is still there, so there might not be much alone time."

She lifted her head and hopped through the cat door. Animals. I swear, no matter how long I lived, I'd never understand them.

"Tea?" my aunt asked.

It was what we liked to do—share a drink. "Of course."

I followed her into the kitchen. "How's Rihanna?" she asked.

I filled her in on the school and how they thought she should do a photo essay on Gerald Plimpton. "I'm worried. He's a definite suspect in the murder of Mr. Hightower."

"Really? How so?"

Darn. I shouldn't have said that. "It's speculation. The sheriff has eliminated Amanda—and I double checked her alibi. Darren's alibi is Olivia, which may or may not be true. I'm running out of people with the motive to kill."

"Just so you know, Darren would never hurt his father."

Considering he and Olivia didn't need to sell the theater —and I bet he'd known that for a while—I'd sort of discounted him too. "I'm sure he wouldn't."

"Who else is on your murder board?"

"Suspect board. We're trying to keep it less threatening for Rihanna."

"Suspect board, it is."

"That's the problem. It's almost empty. I was hoping you had an idea."

She poured the hot water over the teabag. "I wish. I have been talking to the girls, but Pearl said the sheriff is being secretive."

I bet he was. He didn't want to tip off Plimpton. The big question was, what was his plan to catch the guy? Did he think Plimpton would try to take out Darren since he no longer planned to sell?

If he did, Olivia would never buy the old guy out. If only I could read minds, this sleuthing job would be so much easier.

## CHAPTER 18

When I arrived at the office the next morning, I expected to find Rihanna deep into her summer reading. Only she wasn't there, and neither was Jaxson.

"Iggy, where is everyone?"

"I don't know."

"Don't lie." Iggy usually told the truth.

"I'm not. I was asleep when Rihanna left this morning. At least I think that's what happened."

"Fine. Is Sassy here?" She might have seen something.

"No."

"I thought she never left your side?" Nothing seemed to make sense today.

"That's true, but when I woke up, she was gone too."

"Why aren't you doing your happy dance?" He'd been complaining about her not leaving him alone since she arrived on the scene.

He lifted a leg and then set it back down—his way of shrugging. "I've kind of gotten used to her."

Part of me was happy to hear that, but when we solved Mr. Hightower's murder, most likely she'd leave, and I didn't want Iggy to be sad. I looked around. "And where is Aimee? She said she was going to visit you last night."

"She came. She left."

"Did you fight or something?" I asked.

"No."

Something was going on with my familiar, but when he got in one of his moods, he wasn't about to spill the beans. "Fine. I'm going to check Rihanna's room for some clues as to where she might have gone."

Her bed was made—which impressed me—and her backpack was gone. So was her camera equipment. Most likely, Rihanna was out taking photos. Hopefully, she was searching for a replacement for the intriguing looking Mr. Plimpton—or so I wanted to believe.

Since a walk wouldn't hurt me, I decided to check the beach for her. "Tell Jaxson when he comes in that I've gone for a stroll."

"He won't believe me."

I chuckled. "Probably true."

I jotted a note to him saying that I was worried about Rihanna and went looking for her. When I went downstairs, I checked the parking lot to make sure her car was there. It wasn't and that worried me. She had no reason to go to school, so where would she be? Rihanna might have gone to the ice cream shop to interview Mr. Plimpton, assuming he was there, but she wouldn't have driven. Hmm. Most of the places that were of interest in this town were within walking distance, more or less.

To make sure I wasn't being paranoid, I hopped in my car and headed toward the library on the far end of town, all the while keeping an eye out for her vehicle. For all I knew, she was hungry and decided to stop at the store for some food—assuming she had her own money. Then again, why would she when she could eat at the Tiki Hut for free?

I drove about a mile in each direction before deciding I was being overly protective, so I headed back to the office. It wasn't even ten, which meant I shouldn't be worried. Yet.

If she didn't return by late afternoon, I'd call in the cavalry. Upstairs, I found Jaxson.

"Enjoy your walk?" he asked.

"My plans changed. Rihanna's car was gone, so I cruised the streets, but I didn't find her."

He swung his chair around. "She's a big girl. Let's give her the benefit of the doubt and assume she's just enjoying herself."

I could remember back when I was in high school that I'd jump in my car and drive up the coast for the fun of it. There were a lot of cute towns along the way. "You're right."

"Good."

I suppose I could call her, but that seemed over-the-top, even for me. I went over to my desk but realized I had nothing to do. We had no new clients—assuming I didn't count Sassy—and officially we weren't supposed to be investigating Mr. Hightower's murder. "We need an ad campaign to drum up business."

"I agree. Are you good with graphic design?"

"No. My talents do not extend to anything artistic."

Jaxson smiled, though I didn't know why. "Are you good with marketing at least?" he asked.

Why would he think that? "Hardly. I can crunch numbers and do statistical analysis, but that's all. For our company, it's easy. We've had one paying customer. Period. There are no trend lines to draw."

"I see. How do you think we can drum up business?"

How would I know? "Maybe the same way we get our information. We need to use the gossip queens."

"I like it. We could ask Rihanna to maybe take our photo and create some kind of flyer to pass out," he said.

It had potential. "Even if we set up a website, I don't think we can claim victory over any crime. Steve always swoops in and arrests the guilty person. It doesn't seem to matter if we've helped."

He slapped his thighs. "Then word of mouth it is."

He was no help. Even though I was worried about my cousin, I needed something to occupy myself for a few hours. My mother had tried to contact Mr. Hightower, but he didn't seem to want to talk.

I turned around. "Iggy?"

He perked up. "Yes?"

"Is Sassy back yet?"

"When isn't she here?"

"She wasn't here an hour ago. Is she on the sofa?"

"Yes."

I shook my head. Crazy iguana. I figured she was on the left end like before. While I felt a bit self-conscious talking to an empty-looking sofa, she might be our only hope. "Do you think you could try to contact Mr. Hightower for us?"

I looked back at Iggy since he was the only one who could hear her. "She said she could try. What would you like her to ask him?"

I thought it was obvious. "Who killed him? And if he doesn't know, then who gave him the nuts? Was it Mr. Plimpton?"

If Sassy was anything like my mother, she'd need time to make contact, but since Sassy was a ghost, I was hoping she could visit him directly. I suppose I could ask if animal ghosts could talk to people ghosts. If she said no, I'd feel bad, so I left it alone.

While Sassy did her thing, I went over to Jaxson, who smelled really good today, by the way. That was a random thought that I probably should ignore.

"What are you working on?" I asked.

"I'm actually two-timing you. I'm ordering some wine for my brother."

At least one of us was earning money. I had thought about picking up a few shifts at the Tiki Hut Grill, but I'd rather spend time with Rihanna when she wasn't out taking pictures.

Iggy came over. "Sassy isn't having any luck, but she'll keep trying to contact him."

"Thank you, Sassy. I appreciate it. We want to bring the murderer to justice."

"She knows," Iggy said.

Wanting to do something nice for Rihanna, I decided to head to the store and buy her a black bedspread. I was pretty sure she'd appreciate it. Besides, the one I put on her bed was an old one of mine.

I told Jaxson, and he thought it was a good idea. The problem was that even though I love shopping—just not for things that are black—I couldn't stop worrying about my cousin. Once in my car, I caved and called her. It was close to two, and I thought she would have been either hot or tired and ready to come home.

When Rihanna didn't answer, I left her a voicemail and tried not to sound totally stressed out. At some point, I'd have to set up guidelines for how long she could be out and about without leaving a note or sending a text.

After I bought the bedspread and two cute black and white throw pillows, I returned to the office, pretending as if nothing was wrong.

Jaxson wasn't buying my calm demeanor. "No, she's not here, and no, Rihanna hasn't called," he said before I'd even asked the question.

"She'll be back soon, I'm sure. I bet her camera battery will run out of power, and she'll have to return." I had no idea how long those DSLR batteries lasted, nor did I know if she carried a spare. I just wanted to convince myself that she'd be okay.

I calmly changed out the bedspread and checked my phone. Again. No return call. Finally, I couldn't take it any longer. I strode out to the main area. "I'm going to visit Mr. Plimpton to see if Rihanna stopped by his place. She might have told him where she went afterward if she happened to have spoken with him."

Jaxson pushed back his chair. "I'm going with you, and there's no arguing with me."

"What if she comes home in the meantime?"

Jaxson turned to Iggy. "Can you please let our wandering houseguest know to call her cousin immediately?"

"Will do."

"Fine. Let's go."

"Do you know where Plimpton lives in case he's not at the store?"

Darn. My mind had turned into something akin to a ten-year-old ball of string that had been rolling around for years—one with no direction. "No."

Jaxson held up his hand and walked over to his computer. Less than a minute later, he'd written down the address and the directions. "Let's do this."

We stopped first at the ice cream store, but neither Rihanna nor Mr. Plimpton were there. Next, was going to Gerald Plimpton's home. Turns out, it was easy to find. He lived about two miles outside of town, three blocks off the main road. When we arrived, I was disappointed that my cousin's car was not in the driveway. If she had been there, she wasn't now.

Jaxson pulled to a stop on the road. "Do you know what you're going to ask him?"

"Yes. I got this." I pushed open my door before he gave me a lecture about being safe. I had every confidence that Jaxson could take down an elderly man, even if he brandished a gun at us.

I knocked, and while I could hear footsteps, it seemed to take Mr. Plimpton forever to answer. He eventually pulled open the door and stared at me for a moment. "Glinda?"

"Yes, Mr. Plimpton. It's me."

"How can I help you?"

I held up a picture on my phone of Rihanna. "Have you seen this young lady?"

"Why yes. That's Rihanna."

My pulse soared. "She was here then?"

"She sure was. This morning. She showed me some photos she'd taken of me and said she had a school assignment to interview a member of the community. I have to say I was quite flattered."

He sounded sincere. Maybe I had misjudged him. "How long did she stay?"

He looked off to the side. "I don't remember exactly. Maybe an hour and a half. She took a lot more photos and then asked me questions about the ice cream shop." His chin wobbled, looking as if he might cry. "I hadn't thought about those beginning days for a long time. That was when I met Rosie, my wife. Did you know that?"

Everyone had heard that story many times. "Yes. When Rihanna left, did she say where she was going?"

"I don't think so."

I pulled out my business card. "If she calls you or contacts you again, please let me know."

He studied the card, and his face hardened for a moment. "You're a private investigator?"

I thought the title of amateur sleuth was clear. "No. My partner, Jaxson and I, look for lost dogs, missing kids, and spy on unfaithful partners."

Yes, that was a lie, but I wasn't about to say we're looking into Chester Hightower's death and think Mr. Plimpton might be involved.

He waved the card. "I'll be sure to let you know if I see or hear from her."

"Thanks." I was quite dejected when we left.

As soon as I slipped into the car, Jaxson faced me. "He's hiding something."

"Why did you think that?" I usually could spot a liar, but my mental state of late hadn't been in the best shape.

"He kept looking down to the right and then the left every time he tried to recall something. Something about his story is fishy. We need to find Rihanna's car."

"I agree, but do you plan on driving every street in town?"

He twisted toward me. "You're the witch. Can't you do some kind of locator spell?"

I nearly choked. "How do you know about witchcraft?"

"I can use the Internet. There's a ton of stuff there."

He was right. "I've never done a locator spell. I should have tried one when Diana Upton was kidnapped, but it didn't occur to me at the time."

Jaxson started the engine. "No time like the present. Shall we head on over to Hex and Bones Apothecary? I'm sure Bertha can fix you up."

I had nothing to lose. "Sure."

Inside the shop, my anxieties flared. The spells I've attempted had all been important, but none had been a matter of life and death, or at least none that I could remember. Was I being a little dramatic? Sure, but I was in charge of a teenager, and I was failing miserably to keep her safe. Heaven forbid I tell my mother what happened.

I told myself that Rihanna had only been gone seven hours. How much trouble could a teenager get into? For all I knew, she'd met a boy and decided to have a fun day of exploring the Florida beaches.

Jaxson wrapped an arm around my waist and turned me to face him. "Stop obsessing."

My mouth opened. "Can you read minds now? Was that a side effect of one of the spells I put on you?"

"No, but your right eye gets this cute little tick when you're stressing."

He'd been studying me? I wasn't sure I liked it, though it was a bit flattering. "Okay. I'm worried. Happy?"

Before he could answer, Bertha came up to us. "What a pleasant surprise. How can I help you?"

"I need a locator spell."

She didn't answer. Uh-oh. What did that mean?

## CHAPTER 19

"I'm afraid I can't help you with that, Glinda," Bertha said.

"Why not? I know my luck with spells isn't the best, but—"

She held up a hand. "It's not that. A locator spell requires an empath to perform the ceremony."

"I don't understand."

"Come with me, and I'll show you."

We followed her. Because she had an assistant today, she probably felt okay taking us into the back room. We waited while she found a jar of what I would call plain rocks. She then gathered several herbs and spices, carefully checking the jar labels, though for what I don't know. It seemed like a lot of stuff for a demonstration.

Bertha placed four of the rocks across from each other facing north, east, south, and west. "Does the placement of the rocks need to be precise?" I asked.

"No, but you need to spread them out." She then set the spices next to a bowl. "First, I need to mix the dragon's blood sage with strands of the sweet grass sage in order to bring harmony and protection to both you and the person you are trying to locate. That part even you can do."

I almost felt insulted.

"Why did you say we need an empath?" Jaxson asked.

"I'm getting to that. After you light the ingredients and fan the smoke over the rocks, one or two will glow, indicating the direction of the person you seek. But...you won't know where your person is until you place your palms on the glowing rocks."

She wasn't making any sense. "Why not?"

"That's where the empath comes in. There needs to be a strong connection between you and the lost one. Otherwise, you won't be able to get a reading on this person's location."

"But Rihanna is my cousin. I'm kind of her guardian for the next few months."

Bertha's eyes widened, and then she smiled. "Why didn't you say so?"

"Sorry." I didn't know it was part of the equation.

"Then yes, you should be able to do this." She broke up the sage and then added several other ingredients, most of which I'd never heard of before. "When you get home, you need to be surrounded by Rihanna's aura."

"I can sit in her bedroom."

"Perfect. And make sure to keep something dear of hers close by. That will increase your chance of success. Once you are set, light the sage. When the powder catches fire, it will go out quickly, but it will produce a sweet-smelling smoke first. Blow the smoke over the rocks until one or more glow. If one glows, that's the direction where she is. If two glow, she is in between them."

"Will the intensity of the light tell me how far away she is?"

Bertha smiled. "Excellent question, but no. This is where

the connection between you comes in. Place either your hand or hands on the rock or rocks and close your eyes."

"Then what?"

"Focus on your cousin's aura. Concentrate and her location will become known to you."

If I weren't a witch, I'd say this was all hocus pocus. But all of the spells Bertha had shown me had worked—if only for a short while. "Okay."

She looked up at Jaxson. "While Glinda is in Rihanna's room, keep watch outside her door."

I didn't want to ask why. Did she think some spirit would come and whisk me away? I was ashamed at my bad attitude toward the occult. I believed in it, just not when I had to do it.

"Sure."

Once I paid for the materials, she packaged them up, and we headed back to the office. Neither of us said anything on the two-minute trip back, for which I was glad. I was still trying to wrap my head around this. If Rihanna and I didn't have a deep connection, this wouldn't work. To be honest, I don't know if we did or not. We might be related, but my mom and I hadn't kept in touch with my aunt in a while.

Inside, Iggy rushed up to us. "Any news?" he asked.

"Rihanna visited Mr. Plimpton this morning but then left. I'm going to try a locator spell."

"Have you done one before?" my familiar asked.

I could sense doubt, but I shrugged it off. "No, but I'm sure I can figure something out."

Not wanting to listen to any negativity, I did as Bertha instructed. I went into Rihanna's room, while Jaxson stood guard. I set the materials on her desk and looked for something of hers that might have sentimental value. Inside the dresser drawer, I found it. It was a picture of her and her mom when Rihanna was maybe ten. They both looked happy.

I carried the photo over and set it on top of the desk. I then assembled the rocks in the same formation Bertha had shown me. Next, I placed the bowl of magical ingredients in the center. Thankfully, Bertha had included a pack of matches. I inhaled and lit the mixture. Smoke rose immediately, and I coughed. Not good.

Needing to focus, I blew the smoke over the rocks and waited for one of them to glow. I won't lie. When one pulsed orange, I nearly shouted. Succeeding at spells wasn't my norm.

I immediately placed my hand on that rock and focused my attention on what was south of town. I pictured Rihanna smiling as she stood next to her mom. I remembered the cheer in her eyes when she showed me the photos she'd taken.

My stomach grumbled. I was about to dismiss it as me not having eaten in the last few hours, but then I stilled. It might sound silly, but the supermarket was south of here. Had my hunger really been a clue or merely a reality?

Not wanting to jump to conclusions, I kept focused, but no image of my dear cousin appeared. When I opened my eyes, the orange rock had returned to its natural color.

Was that it? Rihanna couldn't have been at the supermarket for the last few hours, right? With nothing else to go on though, I had to investigate. I cleaned up a little, and then pulled open the bedroom door.

Jaxson spun around. "Did you find her?"

He seemed so hopeful, I didn't want to give him false hope. "She might be at the supermarket."

Jaxson dipped his chin, but said nothing for a moment. "You sure?"

"No, but my stomach grumbled during the spell."

He flashed me a quick smile. "Since you're always hungry, I don't think it means much, but I say we check it out anyway."

I'm glad he wanted to see this through with me. "Thank you."

Once more, I told Iggy to have Rihanna call us if she came home.

"Find her, will ya?" Iggy pleaded.

"We will."

Once more, we hopped into Jaxson's car, and he took off toward the supermarket. I tried not to get my hopes up, but I couldn't help it. When we arrived at the store, I swear I almost screamed when I spotted her car. "There."

Jaxson parked close. I jumped out and ran to it. The hood was cold, and to my dismay, the door was unlocked with the keys in the ignition.

Jaxson rushed up next to me. "What is it?"

"Look." I pointed to the keys. "She wouldn't leave them like that."

"Do you think someone kidnapped her?"

I looked around but didn't notice any outside cameras. "Before I jump to any conclusions, let's look inside."

I wasn't hopeful. Jaxson took the east side of the store, and I checked out the west. We looked down every aisle, but Rihanna wasn't there. I walked up to the service counter and explained that my cousin's car was in the lot, but she was nowhere to be found. "Do you have any security cameras inside?"

"Yes, but I'm afraid you'll need a warrant to look at the feed."

"Really?"

"I'm sorry, ma'am."

"Do you have cameras outside?" Just because I hadn't spotted any, it didn't mean they weren't there.

"No."

Darn. Even if I asked Steve to pull the tapes of the inside, and it showed my cousin shopping, it wouldn't tell us who took her afterward—assuming she'd been kidnapped and didn't willingly go someplace.

"Anything?" Jaxson asked.

"No. I'll drive her car back to the office. Okay?"

He rubbed my back, and it helped somewhat. "Are you sure you can drive?"

"Yes." Or so I hoped.

If Rihanna had gone off for the day with a boy and returned to find her car gone, she'd either call me to come get her or have the new friend take her back to the office. I hoped it was something that innocent.

I trudged up the stairs and found Iggy in a state. "What is it? Did Rihanna come home or something?"

"No. Sassy found her."

"Where? How?"

"First question. Rihanna is at Mr. Plimpton's house. Sassy found her tied up in the back bedroom."

I reached out and grabbed Jaxson's arm for support. "Is she okay?" I asked Iggy. That was a dumb question for many reasons, but I wasn't thinking straight.

"He didn't hurt her. Yet."

I swallowed my fear. "Second question. How did Sassy find Rihanna?"

"Mr. Hightower finally contacted her."

This was great news. "What did he say?"

"Gerald."

"He said *Gerald*? That's all?" Iggy nodded. "What about him? Was Mr. Hightower naming his killer or the fact that Rihanna had visited Mr. Plimpton today?"

"I don't know. He just said the name Gerald."

Jaxson lightly touched my arm. "We need to tell Steve."

I faced him. "Tell him what? That a ghost cat told my talking iguana where my cousin is being held hostage?"

"Do you have a better idea?"

Sadly, I did not. "What can the sheriff do?"

"Steve can find some pretense to get inside. I doubt he can get a warrant based on the hearsay of a ghost who contacted his dead owner."

"Fine. I'll go. Want to come?" I'd come to rely on Jaxson more and more. He calmed me somehow.

"Of course."

When we entered the station, Pearl greeted us with a smile that quickly evaporated. "What's wrong?"

"My cousin, Rihanna, has been missing for hours. We found her car abandoned at the supermarket."

"I'll let Steve know you're here." Once she spoke to him, she motioned that we go back.

Steve met us outside his office. "Rihanna is missing?"

I was happy he sounded concerned. "Yes, but we think we know where she is. Only we need your help."

"Come into the office."

It took about ten minutes to detail the events of the last two days, from Rihanna's new guidance counselor suggesting she do a photo essay on Gerald Plimpton to finding her car abandoned in the supermarket parking lot.

"Why do you think she's back at Plimpton's house?"

I inhaled. "You won't believe me."

Steve looked over at Jaxson. "Do you believe her?"

"I do, or rather I believe Iggy. If he said his ghost told him she saw Rihanna tied up in Plimpton's back room, then I believe she is there."

He scrubbed a hand down his jaw. "It's not like I can get a search warrant based on that."

"I know, but maybe Plimpton will let you inside."

He shook his head. "When I spoke to him that one time, I

got the sense he was a wily old codger who wasn't going to be intimidated by the law."

"I'm not going to let him kill her. I'm convinced he murdered Mr. Hightower."

"Based on his dead cat telling you his name?"

I lifted my chin. "Yes."

"Steve," Jaxson said. "What if you head on over and check out his place? If Rihanna is in the back bedroom, I bet you can look through the window and see her. That should be enough to get you inside."

"It would be. I'll take Nash. You escort Glinda home and make sure she doesn't try to interfere." He turned back to me. "If your cousin is there, we'll get her."

"Thank you, but call me when you know something."

"Will do."

Steve pushed back his chair and stood. That was our cue to leave. Once outside, I suggested we have a coffee next door. "I need a pick me up."

"I'm up for that."

This was going to be the longest wait in my life.

## CHAPTER 20

As soon as Miriam spotted us, she rushed over. It appeared as if she'd heard about Rihanna. I guess that happened when Pearl was in the loop.

"How are you two lovebirds today?" she asked.

Heat raced up my face. "We're just--"

Jaxson cut me off. "Great. My partner here is in need of a caffeine fix."

"I have just the thing. And for you, my fit friend?"

Wait? Was I a dumpling or something? I walked. A bit. And thought about exercising.

"A coffee black and something rich and chocolatey. Surprise me."

Now it was Miriam who blushed. I swear Jaxson could sweet talk any woman. As soon as she left to get our order, I checked my watch. "How long do you think Steve and Nash will take?"

"Relax. If Rihanna is in Plimpton's house, they'll get her."

"What if he won't let them in?"

"Let's worry about it if and when the time comes."

Jaxson was right, but I was still upset, mostly because I should have set up some rules with her.

Miriam delivered our food and, for once, didn't ask for or discuss any gossip. Maybe she hadn't heard about Rihanna's possible kidnapping. That was fine by me. I wasn't sure I could discuss what might have happened to my cousin without breaking down.

Jax and I talked about everything but Gerald Plimpton and what he might be capable of. I swear it was hours before my cell rang. "It's Steve." I swiped a finger across the screen. "Yes? Did you find her?"

"We did, and we arrested Gerald Plimpton for the murder of Chester Hightower."

What? My pulse soared with elation, rendering me speechless at the same time. As much as I want to shout out that Rihanna was safe, I didn't need everyone in town to hear it before I had the chance to talk to her. "We'll be right over. And Steve? Thank you."

"I should be thanking your cousin. She got a confession out of Plimpton. When he realized it, he couldn't let her go."

I wasn't able to absorb all of that. "We're on our way over there now."

I pushed back my chair. "Rihanna is safe."

Jaxson threw more than enough cash to cover our order on the table, and we rushed next door. I barely even acknowledged Pearl when we entered. "Where is she?" I asked.

"In the conference room."

I ran and pushed open the door. When I saw my cousin safe and sound, my knees weakened. Rihanna jumped up and hugged me. Or rather I hugged her, maybe a little too hard. I leaned back. "Did he hurt you?"

"Not really. My wrists are a little sore, that's all."

"Have a seat, Glinda," Steve said. "You've got one fine young lady here. She's a real asset."

While I was having a hard time catching my breath, I sat down next to her. Jaxson took the chair on the other side of me. "Tell me everything," I said to Rihanna.

She explained about going to Mr. Plimpton's house to photograph him.

"Didn't you realize he could have killed someone?" I asked.

"Yes, and that's why I recorded everything. My phone eventually ran out of power, but not before I got him to slip up and confess."

"How?"

She looked off to the side for a moment, as if she was debating whether to tell me the truth. "Okay. Don't freak, but I swear I heard him say he killed Mr. Hightower, only his lips weren't moving."

I didn't get it. "How is that possible? I mean, Mom can talk to the dead, but Mr. Plimpton is still alive."

"I can't explain it. It's almost like I read his mind or something. It wasn't a two-way conversation or anything, but when he was telling me about wanting to leave Witch's Cove, I heard such longing that I connected with him."

If she believed it, then maybe it was true. "I trust you didn't confront him?"

"No! I'm not stupid. I asked if I could make him some tea. I needed to get away from him for a minute or two to think what to do."

"It also gave you the chance to look around his house."

She graced me with a quick smile. "That too. Since I believed he'd poisoned Mr. Hightower with the nuts, I thought maybe there was evidence of them lying around. He's not a good housekeeper. In fact, I don't think he's dusted in years."

"Did you find something?" Jaxson asked.

"I did. A nut."

My mind had to work to understand. "As in a Barbados nut?"

"Yes. You guys were talking about it, so I figured this was the poisonous nut that killed Mr. Hightower."

"A bad housekeeper or not, I'm surprised he left it out in the open," Jaxson said.

"He didn't. It was behind a garbage can. I took a photo of it before I moved the can. I picked it up, and after I carried out the tea, I asked him if I could eat it."

I sucked in a breath. "But you knew it was poison." My cousin played a dangerous game.

"I did, but I wanted to see what he'd say. He told me it wasn't ripe and said to throw it in the trash. I returned to the kitchen and pretended to toss it. Instead, I pocketed it."

"I have the evidence now," Steve said.

This was remarkable. I don't think I'd have been able to think on my feet like that. "How did you get him to confess?"

"You'll have to listen to him on tape. He's a lonely old man. Once he started talking about his shop and his wife and how much he wanted to be with his family, he let down his defenses."

"He probably figured that since you were just a kid, you wouldn't be able to do anything about it."

She smiled. "My youthful innocence is my best trait. Mind you, I took out the eyebrow stud before I went there so as not to creep him out."

My cousin was smart. Real smart. "Mr. Plimpton admitted that he gave the nuts to Mr. Hightower?"

"He did."

Steve leaned forward. "I played the tape to Mr. Plimpton afterward, and he had no choice but to sign a confession.

Furthermore, he stated that neither Amanda nor Darren had anything to do with their dad's death."

"That is kind of sad," Rihanna said.

It was a shame that Mr. Plimpton was so desperate that he resorted to murder, but last I looked, it was still a crime to kill someone. "I have one more question. When Jaxson and I came to the door looking for you, did you know we were there?" The house wasn't that big.

"Yes, but he said if I called out that he'd kill you and Iggy, and I couldn't let that happen."

I appreciated her looking out for my familiar. "I trust Mr. Plimpton had no idea that you recorded him, did he?"

Her eyes widened. "No. When he realized he'd said something that would incriminate himself, he made me promise not to tell anyone, which I did. Once I figured a way to get out of there, I planned to tell all."

I smiled. "I am very proud of you for keeping your cool. You are one tough girl."

"Thank you, Glinda."

Jaxson placed his hand on mine and looked over at the sheriff. "Is she free to go?"

"Yes, but I might need to ask her more questions later."

"She'll be at the office, working on her school work for the next few days." There was no way I was letting her out of my sight.

"Of course."

I was so relieved when we finally left. Once we crossed the street, her eyes widened. "My car! I didn't see it at Mr. Plimpton's when the sheriff escorted me out."

I explained that he must have dumped it in the supermarket parking lot. "I did a location spell and found it, so I drove it back here."

"Cool. You did a spell?"

"Yes." I pretended as if that was something I did all the

time. I also implied I was trying to find her car instead of her. In reality, I think it was pure luck that my stomach grumbled when it did. Otherwise, we might never have found her vehicle. I did fess up that it was Sassy who'd found her—with the help of Mr. Hightower.

"Thank you for everything," she said.

"Of course. I won't lie and say that you didn't give us a scare."

"I know. I'm sorry."

I believed her too.

Upstairs, the moment she spotted Iggy, she picked him up and hugged him. "I'm so glad you're okay."

Iggy licked her face. "Me? I wasn't in danger. Are you okay?"

"Yes."

"I want to hear all about your adventure," Iggy said.

"How about letting Rihanna clean up before she has to tell her story again?" I suggested.

"Okay."

Rihanna set him down and rushed off to clean up. Exhausted, I dropped down onto the sofa. "Is Sassy here?" I asked Iggy.

"Yes."

"Please tell her thank you for finding Rihanna. I will be forever in her debt." I then remembered that I could tell her myself. "You're welcome to stay for as long as you wish, Sassy." Wherever you are.

He tilted his head. What could I say? She'd been a huge help.

Iggy faced the sofa and then turned back to me. "She said she has to go soon. With Mr. Hightower's murder solved, she wants to be with him."

My heart almost cracked at the sentiment. "I understand." I turned to Jaxson. "You know, with both of our cases solved, we should celebrate."

"I'm always up for that."

"How about if we have a *crossing over the rainbow bridge party*. Whoever has lost a pet can bring a photo of him or her, and we'll celebrate."

He grinned. "Why Glinda Goodall, I didn't know you were such a softy."

If he wasn't sitting a few feet away from me, I would have punched him.

The next two days were hectic. I barely saw Rihanna, because she was holed up in her room. She claimed she was excited to write up her story about helping to solve Chester Hightower's murder.

"Don't worry," Rihanna said. I'm not going to mention the part about hearing voices, because everyone would think I'm weird."

"That's probably smart, at least until you learn who you can trust."

Even though I grew up in Witch's Cove, where witches were the norm, I didn't talk much about what I could or couldn't do. That was partly because I didn't think I could do anything very well.

Personally, I wasn't surprised at Rihanna's talent. Her mother could talk to the dead, but I've always suspected my mother is capable of being a bit of a psychic. Aunt Tricia never embraced her witch side, but that didn't mean she didn't have talent. As for Rihanna's dad, he passed away when she was one. I heard mention of him being a warlock, but no one ever talked about it after he passed.

A knock sounded on our office door and then my mom

came in carrying a huge box. I rushed over. "Here, let me help you."

"Thanks." Sweat beaded on her forehead.

"What is all this?"

"I know Fern is helping with the catering, as is Drake, but we need decorations for the party."

My heart sank. My mom's idea of decorations scared me. "You didn't have to."

"I wanted to. Put it down on the coffee table and help me unpack."

Jaxson came upstairs carrying a box of what I could only guess was wine. "Hey, Wendy." He nodded to her box. "Need help."

"Yes."

Mom smiled and pulled out a rolled-up sheet of plastic. Oh, no. It was a rainbow, just like in *The Wizard of Oz*. The edges were a bit tattered, and the colors faded. "How old is this?" I asked.

"I got this for your first birthday party. You don't remember?"

Seriously? "Must have slipped my mind."

She turned to Jaxson. "Can you help me tack it up?"

He grinned. The man infuriated me sometimes. He knew all this movie memorabilia drove me crazy. I might have objected to having the rainbow above my desk had this not been about crossing over the rainbow bridge. I wanted to honor not only Sassy, but all of the other animals who were now in a better place.

After they hung the banner, I thought she was finished, but no. She dragged out some speakers and placed her phone in the slot. I knew what was coming. While I thought Judy Garland did a great job with the song *Somewhere Over The Rainbow*, the thought of it on an infinite loop might make me want to join those animals.

Iggy came over. "That's great, Wendy," he said.

I squinted at him. I'd always demanded that he treat my mom with respect and call her Mrs. Goodall.

She turned around and smiled. "Thank you, Iggy. I'm glad to see someone appreciates my good taste."

Jaxson winked at me. It was at that moment I decided it might be time to let go of my rule of never dating a coworker. What that man did to my soul should be outlawed.

Rihanna emerged from her cave with a smile on her face. She took one look at the rainbow and sucked in a breath, a look of horror quickly crossing her face. Oh, yes. That girl and I were so going to get along just fine.

# EXCERPT- GONE IN THE PINK OF AN EYE

I hope you enjoyed seeing how Glinda and Jaxson handled their first case for The Pink Iguana Sleuth company. In book 6, Rihanna becomes involved in yet another case.

Gone in The Pink of an Eye (book 6 of A Witch's Cove Mystery) is available.

Buy on Amazon or read for FREE on Kindle Unlimited

*Don't forget to sign up for my Cozy Mystery* newsletter *to learn about my discounts and upcoming releases. If you prefer to only receive notices regarding my releases, follow me on BookBub.*

**A dead body on the beach and no suspects. Not the way a sleuth should start her day.**

Hi, I'm Glinda Goodall, part-time waitress and part-time sleuth. Oh yeah, I'm a witch with a talking pink iguana who thinks he's a detective.

A few weeks ago, my seventeen-year-old cousin moved in with me (long story). Her passion? Taking photos. She's a witch too, but she refuses to acknowledge it—until she starts to hear voices in her head.

When the dead man turns out to be her photo teacher, I have to help her find out who killed him. This obsession to learn his identity forces Rihanna to embrace her witch side, which leads to seances, ghost sightings, and a whole host of paranormal explorations—and I end up wearing something other than pink. Not a pretty sight.

Please stop by The Pink Iguana Sleuth agency if you need anything. Either Jaxson or I will be there—and Iggy, of course.

**Here is Chapter 1:**

"I had the best week of my life," my seventeen-year-old cousin, Rihanna, announced, and I couldn't have been happier. Before I explain why, I need to mention how she came to even be here with me.

Jaxson Harrison, my partner in our newly formed company, The Pink Iguana Sleuths, and I were at the Tiki Hut Grill with Rihanna Samuels to celebrate her rather unexpected move from Jacksonville, Florida to Witch's Cove a few weeks ago.

Why unexpected? My aunt Tricia—Rihanna's mother—had been going through a hard time with substance abuse, when she suddenly decided to enter rehab. While my mom and I were elated she finally took this big step to recovery, she refused to say what had prompted the change.

And as fantastic as that event was, it meant someone had to watch her daughter—make that her rather rebellious teenaged daughter—or so her mother claimed.

I, on the other hand, found these last few weeks with Rihanna to have been wonderful. Like any teenager, though, she would take off without notice and not check in. While that worried me sick, she did help solve a murder case! Not bad for a kid.

Let me take a step back. When she showed up on our doorstep, our biggest hurdle had been to figure out where she was going to sleep. My apartment was only a one-bedroom, and my parents' living quarters above the mortuary didn't have a spare room. With a bit of work, Jaxson and I managed to clear a space at the back of our office and convert it into a bedroom. That meant Rihanna kind of became part of our sleuth agency, mostly because the walls were really thin, allowing her to overhear many of our conversations. It was how she was able to insert herself into our last investigation—against our wishes. But as I said, she did help solve the case.

Fast forward a few weeks, and it brings us to now. We were at dinner to celebrate her first week of school.

"What was the best part of your week?" Jaxson asked my cousin.

He always seemed to know when I was spacing out. *Thank you, Jaxson, for picking up the slack.*

"My photojournalism teacher is amazing. I can't believe he went to Iraq to take photos. Talk about dangerous. Not only that, he's traveled all over the US—to New York, Chicago, and Los Angeles. He's been everywhere."

I wonder how Witch's Cove, Florida, a town with a population of two thousand, managed to snag him? "What a resumé. What's his name?" I asked.

For the record, mine is Glinda Goodall. And yes, my mom named me after Glinda the Good Witch from the South, probably because I am a witch—and because she is obsessed with the movie *The Wizard of Oz*. My mom's a witch too. But enough about us for now.

"Mr. Tillman. The guy is a genius. He gets people. I mean, I swear his shots expose a person's soul."

"That's wonderful. When I went to Witch's Cove High School, there was no class like that," I said.

"Not when I went either," Jaxson added.

Jaxson is six years older than me, and I'm almost twenty-seven. While we attended the same school, I only met him because his younger brother, Drake, was my best friend. Back then, Jaxson was trouble—big time. Now? He's a real sweetie.

"One reason I am so stoked is because I made an A on my photo essay. It's the one I did on Mr. Plimpton."

Ah, yes. Good old Mr. Plimpton, the man from our last case. He was desperate to sell his ice cream shop, which he eventually did, not that it would do him any good now (long story).

"An A? Wow, that's fantastic. How about your other classes?" I asked.

Before I go on, I have to confess that I love math, and yes, I know I'm in the minority. While I didn't like teaching middle school math, I loved the subject.

"You mean math?" she asked with a smile, knowing full well that that was where I shone.

"Yes, like math." I cared about history and science and stuff, but math was the end all to be all.

"I made a C+ on my first quiz."

"That's…good."

"For me it is. Trigonometry isn't my thing."

"I can help, you know."

"I know, but I want to figure things out for myself."

"I can respect that."

Jaxson slightly nudged me under the table. I shouldn't have brought up the subject of grades, but I wanted her to succeed. Rihanna was a very independent girl and could achieve anything she set her mind to, but she could sometimes lose focus about what was important in life—like staying safe. However, I don't blame her for not wanting my help. "Great. Have you made any friends?"

She dipped her head. "Like witch friends or normal people friends?"

"Ouch." Just because her mom never practiced witchcraft and her warlock dad passed away when Rihanna was only one year old, it didn't mean she hadn't inherited some talent. Just two weeks ago, she'd heard a killer's thoughts. It was real psychic stuff. I certainly don't possess that kind of ability—at least not that I was aware of.

"Sorry," she said, though from the tilt of her head, she wasn't sorry at all.

"You're welcome to invite anyone over to the office, even after Jaxson and I have gone home for the night." I would not give her *the talk*. I could only hope her mom had already done so. "Just make sure everything is picked up by morning in case a client stops by."

"I will, and thanks."

I suppose I'd find out who my cousin hung out with if and only if she invited them back to the office when we were there, of course.

"Anything else notable happen the first week of your senior year?" I asked. "Like some cute guy asked to sit next to you at lunch?"

She shrugged. "Hardly. To be honest, I'd rather be outside taking pictures than sitting in class."

"I get it."

She glanced between me and Jaxson. "You mentioned clients. Anyone interesting?"

Our lack of clients was a sensitive topic, and she knew it. Since opening our agency a little while ago, we'd had one paying customer. Thankfully, Jaxson still worked at his brother's wine and cheese emporium located on the first floor of our building to earn some money. While I didn't often pick up a shift at the Tiki Hut Grill, I did so when needed. "No. I meant in case we land a client, I would appreciate it if you made sure the place was presentable by morning."

"Got it."

Just in time, our food arrived, and I dug in. My Aunt Fern, who owed the Tiki Hut grill, was at the cash register and kept looking our way, though I'm not sure what she expected to see. Fireworks? Between whom?

Before I could decipher her look, the front door to the restaurant whooshed open and Dr. Elissa Sanchez, our medical examiner, breezed in with a young man who looked vaguely familiar.

Rihanna's fork froze in mid-air as she stared at him, acting rather star-struck. For the first time since she'd arrived, she seemed interested in someone her own age. Her last two crushes had been when she met Jaxson, and then again when we ran into our sheriff.

"Who is he?" Rihanna whispered.

"I don't know, but the woman with him is our medical examiner."

"I would have noticed if he went to my high school."

"Give me a sec." Did I mention it's in my DNA to meddle?

Rihanna's eyes widened, and then she grabbed my wrist. "What are you doing?"

"Don't worry." She acted as if I was going to charge over to Dr. Sanchez's table and ask for an introduction. I didn't need to. I had a better source.

When she let go, I pushed back my chair, and walked over to my aunt—one of the five gossip queens of Witch's Cove.

"Glinda? What's up?" she asked, knowing full well I was looking for the scoop on something.

"Who's the handsome young man with Dr. Sanchez?" When I recognized that glint in her eyes, I held up my hand.

"Don't worry, I'm asking for Rihanna. Sheesh. He's way too young for me."

"Whew. That is a relief. How is that going with your hot man?"

This wasn't about me and Jaxson. "Good, now about the young man in question?"

She grinned. "You can't fool me. I see the way you look at your *partner*," Aunt Fern said.

"Shh." She talked too loud. "Jaxson is my *business* partner, but it might turn into something more. In time. When I'm ready. And assuming no one meddles."

My aunt winked. "I get it. Slow and easy it is. The young man in question is Gavin Sanchez, Elissa's son."

"Mom never mentioned the M.E. had a son."

"He spends a lot of time with his dad, who's a lawyer in Miami. Gavin goes to a boarding school down there, but he just graduated from high school. I believe your mother told me he plans to do a gap year and study with his mom. He wants to become a doctor."

"That's admirable. Rihanna will be happy to hear that. Thank you, dear Aunt."

She laughed. "Go back to your man. By the way, he hasn't taken his eyes off you."

I doubted that. I spun around and returned to the table not wanting to know why Jaxson was indeed watching me.

Rihanna dabbed her mouth with a napkin and held it there. "So?"

Since she was facing the hunky teenager, she probably feared he'd know she was talking about him. "His name is Gavin Sanchez. He's about eighteen and will be taking this next year off to study medical examiner stuff with his mom."

"A year to study dead people? Wow. He must be smart. And dedicated."

The longing in her voice implied she liked the intelligent

type. Good. "I'm not surprised, considering his mom is a doctor and his dad is a lawyer. From what I recall, his folks divorced a long time ago though. His grandparents, Betty and Frank Sanchez own the Candles Bookstore. I bet he'll stop in there now and again." I couldn't help myself from sharing everything I knew.

The joy in her eyes was obvious. Ten bucks says it wouldn't take long before those two accidentally ran into each other. I was positive she'd draw Gavin's attention. My cousin was hard to miss. Rihanna was model thin, five feet ten inches tall, and had long, straight black hair. Did I mention she's gorgeous? Okay, I might be a little prejudice, but she was striking—even with the black lipstick and black eye makeup. I figure the nose stud and eyebrow piercing might attract the younger crowd. It made her mysterious looking, for sure.

Rihanna lowered her napkin. "Thanks," she said with a grin.

Once we finished our celebration dinner, I turned to something else that was weighing on my mind. Money. I mentally ran through which shifts I wanted to pick up in order to have some cash available should the need arise. Drake might not be charging us rent, but we had to pay for utilities. Not to mention, feeding Rihanna would cost something. Aunt Fern said my cousin was welcome to eat at the Tiki Hut for free, but I didn't think that was fair to my aunt.

Working mornings would give me the afternoon off, but the evening shift would allow me to sleep in. Considering no one had died recently, and we didn't have any paying customers, I didn't see the need to sit in the office all day doing nothing. To ensure we didn't miss a potential client though, we had a sign on the outside that said to call either Jaxson or myself should we be out and about.

"Time to get you home," I said.

We walked Rihanna back to our office where she was staying.

"You know I could have walked the hundred feet by myself," Rihanna reminded us.

"I know, but it's nice out, and I'm not ready to call it a night yet." The salted sea air coming off the Gulf of Mexico always soothed my soul.

We reached the steps that led up to the second floor office. "Then I'll say thank you and goodnight. I have some reading to do. And yes, I'll look over my Trig again to see why I botched the quiz."

On a Friday night? She acted too much like me. "Good for you. If you have time, you could call your mom."

That had been a sore subject. I think Rihanna wanted to pretend as if she hadn't grown up with a single mother who basically chose to avoid life through drugs.

"I will. Someday. When I'm ready."

She really did sound like me. I know my mother had called her sister a few times since Rihanna's arrival to let her know how well her daughter was adapting, but getting a call from her only child might help with her recovery.

Once Rihanna was safely inside, I turned to Jaxson. "Thanks for joining us."

"You know I'm always up for a free meal."

I chuckled. It hadn't been free for me. "See you tomorrow then?"

"Yup. Are you going to work at the office or at the restaurant?"

"I think I'll do a little organizing at the office first. Then I might pick up an evening shift."

He clasped my shoulders, leaned over, and kissed my forehead. "Night, pink lady."

My heart dropped to my stomach before slowly bouncing back again. I was sure his gesture was platonic but having his large body close to mine did something to my insides. "Night," I managed to choke out.

So you're in the loop, the pink lady nickname referred to the fact that I only wear pink. Rihanna, on the other hand, only wears black.

As Jaxson slid into his car, I headed back to my apartment that was situated above the restaurant. On my very short walk back, my cell rang, but I didn't recognize the number. "Hello?"

"Is this The Pink Iguana Sleuth Agency?"

"Yes, it is." My hands actually shook. Could this be a client? We'd done nothing to warrant a complaint.

"My name is Isobel Holt. Two days ago, my house was broken into."

I hadn't heard. "I'm so sorry. How can I help?"

"The sheriff is investigating the theft, but he says he has no leads. One of the items stolen was a very sentimental piece of jewelry that belonged to my mother. I'll pay whatever you charge to get it back."

I was almost about to say I was pretty good at finding murderers, but I that had no experience with thieves. Fortunately, my filter remained in place. "We'd be happy to help. Can you stop by the office tomorrow morning? Say at nine?"

"I'll be there. And thank you."

I practically skipped home. We had our second client! Things were definitely looking up for The Pink Iguana Sleuths.

Gone in The Pink of an Eye (book 6 of A Witch's Cove Mystery) is available.

Buy on Amazon or read for FREE on Kindle Unlimited

THE END

## ABOUT THE AUTHOR

Love it HOT and STEAMY? Sign up for my newsletter and receive MONTANA DESIRE for FREE. Click here

OR Are you a fan of quirky PARANORMAL COZY MYSTERIES? Sign up for this newsletter. Click Here

Not only do I love to read, write, and dream, I'm an extrovert. I enjoy being around people and am always trying to understand what makes them tick. Not only must my romance books have a happily ever after, I need characters I can relate to. My men are wonderful, dynamic, smart, strong, and the best lovers in the world (of course).

My Paranormal Cozy Mysteries are where I let my imagination run wild with witches and a talking pink iguana who believes he's a real sleuth.

I believe I am the luckiest woman. I do what I love and I have a wonderful, supportive husband, who happens to be hot!

**Fun facts about me**
(1) I'm a math nerd who loves spreadsheets. Give me numbers and I'll find a pattern.
(2) I live on a Costa Rica beach!
(3) I also like to exercise. Yes, I know I'm odd.

I love hearing from readers either on FB or via email (hint, hint).

**Social Media Sites**

**Website**: www.velladay.com
**FB**: www.facebook.com/vella.day.90
**Twitter**: velladay4
**Gmail**: velladayauthor@gmail.com
**Tiktok**: Velladayauthor1
Bookbub: https://www.bookbub.com/authors/vella-day

## ALSO BY VELLA DAY

**THE TIME TRAVEL TALISMAN COZY MYSTERY** (Cozy Mystery)
The Knitting Conundrum (book 1)
The Knitting Dilemma (book 2)
The Knitting Enigma (book 3)
The Knitting Quandary (book 4)

**A WITCH'S COVE MYSTERY** (Paranormal Cozy Mystery)
PINK Is The New Black (book 1)
A PINK Potion Gone Wrong (book 2)
The Mystery of the PINK Aura (book 3)
Box Set (books 1-3)
Sleuthing In The PINK (book 4)
Not in The PINK (book 5)
Gone in the PINK of an Eye (book 6)
Box Set (books 4-6)
The PINK Pumpkin Party (book 7)
Mistletoe with a PINK Bow (book 8)
The Magical PINK Pendant (book 9)
Box Set (books 7-9)
The Poisoned PINK Punch (book 10)
PINK Smoke and Mirrors (book 11)
Broomsticks and PINK Gumdrops (book 12)
Box Set (books 10-12)
Knotted Up In PINK Yarn (book 13)

Ghosts and PINK Candles (book 14)

Pilfered PINK Pearls (book 15)

Box Set (books 13-15)

The Case of the Stolen PINK Tombstone (book 16)

The PINK Christmas Cookie Caper (book 17)

PINK Moon Rising (book 18)

Box set(books 16-18)

The PINK Wedding Dress Whodunit (book 19)

**SILVER LAKE SERIES (3 OF THEM)**
**<u>A TASTE OF SILVER LAKE</u>**
**Weres and Witches Box Set (books 1-2)**
**Hidden Realms Box Set (books 1-2)**
**Goddesses of Destiny Box Set (books 1-2)**

(1). **<u>HIDDEN REALMS OF SILVER LAKE</u>** (Paranormal Romance)

Awakened By Flames (book 1)

Seduced By Flames (book 2)

Box Set (books 1-2)

Kissed By Flames (book 3)

Destiny In Flames (book 4)

Box Set (books 3-4)

Passionate Flames (book 5)

Ignited By Flames (book 6)

Box Set (books 5-6)

Touched By Flames (book 7)

Bound By Flames (book 8)

Box set (books 7-8)

Fueled By Flames (book 9)

Scorched By Flames (book 10)
Box Set (books 9-10)

(2). **GODDESSES OF DESTINY** Paranormal Romance)

Slade (book 1)
Rafe (book 2)
Will (book 3)
Josh (book 4)
Jace (book 5)
Tanner (book 6)

(3). **WERES AND WITCHES OF SILVER LAKE** (Paranormal Romance)

A Magical Shift (book 1)
Catching Her Bear (book 2)
Surge of Magic (book 3)
The Bear's Forbidden Wolf (book 4)
Box Set (books 1-4)

Her Reluctant Bear (book 5)
Freeing His Tiger (book 6)
Protecting His Wolf (book 7)
Waking His Bear (book 8)
Box Set (books 5-8)
Melting Her Wolf's Heart (book 9)
Her Wolf's Guarded Heart (book 10)
His Rogue Bear (book 11)
Reawakening Their Bears (book 12)
Box Set (books 9-12)

## OTHER PARANORMAL SERIES

**PACK WARS** (Paranormal Romance)
Training Their Mate (book 1)
Claiming Their Mate (book 2)
Rescuing Their Virgin Mate (book 3)
Box Set (books 1-3)
Loving Their Vixen Mate (book 4)
Fighting For Their Mate (book 5)
Enticing Their Mate (book 6)
Box Set (books 4-6)
Their Huntress Mate (book 7)
Craving Their Mate (book 8)

**PACK WARS-THE GRANGERS**
Meant for them (book 1)
Meant for wolves (book 2)
Meant for forever (book 3)
Meant for her (book 4)
Meant for two (book 5)

**HIDDEN HILLS SHIFTERS** (Paranormal Romance)
An Unexpected Diversion (book 1)
Bare Instincts (book 2)
Shifting Destinies (book 3)
Embracing Fate (book 4)
Promises Unbroken (book 5)

Bare 'N Dirty (book 6)

Hidden Hills Shifters Complete Box Set (books 1-6)

## CONTEMPORARY SERIES

**MONTANA PROMISES** (Full length contemporary Romance)

Promises of Mercy (book 1)

Foundations For Three (book 2)

Montana Fire (book 3)

Montana Promises Box Set (books 1-3)

Hart To Hart (Book 4)

Burning Seduction (Book 5)

Montana Promises Complete Box Set (books 1-5)

Novellas:

Montana Desire (book 1)

Awakening Passions (book 2)


**PLEDGED TO PROTECT** (contemporary romantic suspense)

From Panic To Passion (book 1)

From Danger To Desire (book 2)

From Terror To Temptation (book 3)


**BURIED SERIES** (contemporary romantic suspense)

Buried Alive (book 1)

Buried Secrets (book 2)

Buried Deep (book 3)

The Buried Series Complete Box Set (books 1-3)


**A NASH MYSTERY** (Contemporary Romance)

Sidearms and Silk(book 1)

Black Ops and Lingerie(book 2)

A Nash Mystery Box Set (books 1-2)

**STARTER SETS (Romance)**

Contemporary

Paranormal

Printed in Great Britain
by Amazon